To Kill a Matzo Ball

To Kill a Matzo Ball

Delia Rosen

KENSINGTON PUBLISHING CORP.

http://www.kensingtonbooks.com

KENSINGTON BOOKS are published by

Kensington Publishing Corp.
119 West 40th Street
New York, NY 10018

All Kensington Titles, Imprints, and Distributed Lines are
available at special quantity discounts for bulk purchases
for sales promotions, premiums, fund-raising, and ed-
ucational or institutional use. Special book excerpts or
customized printings can also be created to fit specific
needs. For details, write or phone the office of the
Kensington special sales manager: Kensington Publishing Corp., 119 West 40th Street, New York, NY 10018,
attn: Special Sales Department, Phone: 1-800-221-2647.

Kensington and the K logo Reg. U.S. Pat & TM Off.

ISBN-13: 978-0-7582-8201-9
ISBN-10: 0-7582-8201-X
First Kensington Mass Market Edition: July 2014

eISBN-13: 978-0-7582-8202-6
eISBN-10: 0-7582-8202-8
First Kensington Electronic Edition: July 2014

10 9 8 7 6 5 4 3 2 1

Printed in the United States of America

To Kill a Matzo Ball

Chapter 1

Viv, my mother's first cousin—my first cousin once removed—used to be in the music business, sort of. She purchased records, vinyl records, real records, for a major chain and used to bring me 45 rpm singles when I was a little girl. Artists like Prince, Gloria Estefan, and Madonna.

"This one is twenty-two with a bullet or seventeen without a bullet," she used to say.

I loved that phrase. It sounded so strong, better than anything I could think of, like "twenty-two on an elevator" or "seventeen with a kite tail."

It was a dramatic expression, though much less so when there was a twist to it. In my case, that twist was a matzo ball.

But I get ahead of myself.

It had been fourteen months and three weeks since I'd left my evaporating clientele on Wall Street to take over Murray's Deli, the establishment founded by my uncle in Nashville.

My estranged father lived with him in a typically irresponsible effort to find himself. He never did that, but without my mother and me, he was free to discover daily diversions. With both my parents gone, there was no one to inherit but me.

Leaving New York for Tennessee was like the migration of my forebears to Palestine at the turn of the last century. When the Next Year in Jerusalem crowd got there and found swamps, malaria, heat, angry Bedouins, and sand, they puzzled over what had *seemed* like a sterling idea just a few months before. When you leave Manhattan Island you leave a city where you can see a black man ask directions from an Orthodox Jew (and get them), where a mosque and a church can exist on the same block, where *clan* means your family. And where the first cop you meet doesn't ask you on a date and become one of your first exes.

I have an ex-husband in New York, but after we split I didn't see him, except at shindigs of mutual friends. If you run a restaurant in a much smaller city, if you help solve crimes— more on which in a minute—you see people you want to see, don't want to see, don't know, don't want to know, or don't have the time or energy to know. You have a staff, which fulfills whatever need you have to socialize and wallow in second-hand drama. Nearing the twilight of my thirties, I prefer to experience that kind of stimulation passively, on my TV or in a paperback novel . . . not in my face.

Then there's crime.

Maybe I carried the New York City rhythm down south with me, distilled and compacted and served up in a trio of murders that eerily found their way into my life. One of them literally dropped in on me, through the ceiling of a party I was catering. Another drove up to my back door when a bread delivery man was murdered in his truck. A third happened down the street, where a customer was killed after eating poisoned herring.

Coincidences? Maybe. When you're in a service industry where you meet a lot of people, chances are some of them are going to die. Suddenly. Violently. Three in less than a year might seem like lottery-sized odds, but then there *are* people who win those things. Maybe I'm just unlucky in love, lucky in death. I am not religious, and I'm spiritual only to the extent that if the receipts are bad for a few days I say a quiet, informal prayer or yell at the Almighty—depending on my mood. I don't believe in karma or that my past misdeeds make me a magnet for crazy people.

But it *is* just a little weird how many corpses I've been introduced to since moving into my uncle's modest home outside Nashville with my two cats. Remarkably, my loyal little staff did not seem unduly surprised or shaken by the events of the last year-plus. Thomasina, my manager, who was also devoted to my uncle, is my rock. *She's* religious, so I guess I get secondhand grace.

My kitchen help—Newt cooks, and Luke busses and occasionally cooks—are young in every sense of the word. Luke, an aspiring rock-and-roller, is dating the pierced and tatted young Dani, who is part of my diligent waitstaff. She is my only personal hire, having walked in at the right time on the right day. She is a good if not exceptional waitperson, but she is terrific at managing our Facebook page, something that is way beyond my area of experience or interest. Her coworkers are the older Raylene and A.J., veterans of Uncle Murray. A.J.'s collegiate daughter, A.J. Two, also works for me as a floating waitperson when she is home from college. I could use another me. But even if I could find someone who had my peculiar mix of dedication and masochism—how else would you describe a non-people-person working long hours in a people-oriented business?—I probably couldn't afford her or him. As my uncle used to say when I came down for one of my rare visits, the store does a comfortable business. That's Jewish for "a little above break-even."

I've always meant to keep track of how many customers are regulars, how many are tourists, how many try to eat healthy, and how many don't care. I eyeball it and have a rough idea, but never enough to actually formulate business-building programs—loyalty cards for regulars, discounts for first-timers, healthy menus to steal patrons from the rabbit holes that serve carrots and lettuce. You know: an actual business plan like the ones I urged my clients to have when I worked on Wall Street. Like so many good and necessary intentions in my life, in any life, this one stays in the to-do pile under a paperweight called "responsibilities." Keeping things running up front, taking inventory, ordering everything from meat to bread to vegetables to coffee filters, chatting with vendors just long enough not to seem rude, hand-holding staff when they're upset—it's all time-consuming and tiring. I don't wear a *shmate* on my head because it's stylish: I haven't had time to see my hairstylist Amanda for weeks. A transplanted New Jerseyite, she's the farthest-north person I know down here. Everyone else is either local or from somewhere in the South.

It's a different world than the one in which I grew up.

Incredibly, it's also a louder one.

Monday-morning breakfast is the busiest time of the week for Murray's Deli. People down here tend to stay up late on Sunday, sucking the last bit of recreation or barhopping from the weekend. That means Caffeine Mondays. We don't do deliveries, but we do a lot of takeout so people can eat in their cars, parks, or offices. I import our coffee from a place in Greenwich Village I used to frequent, and, frankly, it's the best in New York, which makes it the best in Nashville. People literally line up for a super-large cuppa every Monday morning or plop themselves at the counter if there's an open space. Eat-in refills are free. That was something I swore I'd change after students started coming in and caffeine-ing up while they worked. Then Newt suggested I just kill the wireless service for two minutes. The freeloaders were gone in a flash.

This particular morning, there was a customer at the counter I didn't recognize. He sat in the far corner, away from the counter where Thomasina controlled the cash register, the seating, the staff, and anything else required of her capable hands. The only time I ever saw her stymied was when we had some witches to deal with . . . but that's another story. Literally.

I was busy in my usual job as a "floater." I back up everyone, including Newt on the grill and Luke bussing, even Thomasina, if need be. At the heart of the rush, Thomasina pointed out the guy, who had a bran muffin and coffee and then more coffee and just occupied space after that as he worked on his laptop. In addition to the coffee line, there was a line of people waiting to get in. Weekends were a big tourist time, and we saw a lot of RV types looking to fuel up before they headed home farther south. And laptop-man was holding a valuable piece of real estate.

I walked over, intending to do the usual drill. Even though the check was sitting beside his plate, I was going to ask if he needed anything else.

The customer turned toward me when I was still a few steps away. He had a narrow face with a strong chin. The lines of his cheek, framed by collar-length graying hair, all said fiftysomething. He smiled wryly. It was a gentle smile—not amused, not mocking, just disarming.

"No thanks. I'm good," he said in a voice as smooth as egg cream, then went back to tippy-typing on his laptop with all ten fingers.

"I'm glad," I said. Now, it shouldn't take Kreskin to know why someone in an apron and with her brown hair pulled back and a look of unsympathetic resolve was coming to talk to him. And given that he was well-dressed in a light gray suit and thin red tie, and knew how to type, I guessed he was a professional something. Not stupid. "Thing is, if you're done we really could use the stool."

The man turned his pale blue eyes on me. "I'll buy something else," he said.

I took my pad from where I wore it like a six-shooter. My hip was cocked, and so was my mouth. I was prepared for, "*I'll have tea*" or "*Make me a sandwich to go. I'll sit here till it's ready*" and my brain was already replying with, "*There's a three-buck minimum for counter service*" and "*Would you mind waiting at the counter?*"

The man turned back to his laptop. "Please bring me whatever you care to serve. Thank you."

I wasn't expecting that. "Care to give me a food group?"

He thought for a moment. "Yang."

"Sorry?"

"Excuse me, that's dairy or meat," he smiled. "I forget sometimes."

Forget what? That you're among humans? "I assume there's 'yin' food? Greens?"

"Basically, yes," he replied.

"I've got some cottage cheese that's about to expire . . ."

"Perfect."

". . . and milk I was gonna take home to the cats."

"Very fine," he said, almost eagerly.

I pride myself on our menu, but clearly the man wasn't here for the cuisine. I looked at his laptop. There were graphs and—talk about full circle—they were the kind I remembered seeing in a recording studio Viv once took me to, little green bars bouncing up and down showing audio levels.

"They're waves," he said, anticipating my question.

"What kind?"

"Astral," he replied. "Mostly from inside, a few from the street."

Oh. One of those. "I'll get your order," I said and turned.

"Great. I'll be interested to see how that impacts the readings."

"Food?" I said. I was no physicist, but I knew that food was pretty inert, unless there was garlic overkill like those schmucks did to everything at The Pesh House down the street. "How do you measure food waves?"

"With my body. Food, and also certain kinds of minerals."

"I see. They get to the computer program how?"

"I'm my own Wi-Fi," he replied.

Okay. Now, ninety percent of the people who walk through the doors of the deli I inherited are what you would describe as "normal." They're generally pleasant and are pretty courteous. Roughly nine percent are a little wacky. Like the wiccans I mentioned earlier; they had tattoos of body parts on their flesh, and they cast spells. One regular wants the condiments removed from the table, says he doesn't believe he should add anything that isn't in the original recipe. Another regular orders breakfast for lunch, dinner for breakfast, that sort of thing. Swears it keeps her digestive tract on its toes. One of our customers puts the plate on his lap and imagines he's at home watching TV. Says that stimulates his imagination.

They're all harmless. Maybe this guy was too. But it's always best to ask a few more questions to see which way the crazy is blowing.

"Is this something you've trained yourself to do?" I asked.

"It's latent in all of us, one of the nine bodily planes," he answered. "The bars blipped up a little when you came over and we made a connection on the astral plane."

"Did it?"

He hit a button and the graphs scanned backward in fast motion. He was right: as the time stamp went backward a minute, the bars dropped.

"You're saying I caused that?" I asked.

"*We* did," he gently corrected me. "The astral plane is where humans interconnect. Since I'm a trained transmitter, it showed up on the monitor."

He touched a key, and the bars went back to the present readings. "So—and forgive the interruption—"

"Not at all. It's fascinating to watch the bars climb a little the longer you're here."

"What is so important about you being here?"

"The crowd," he said. "I go from group gathering to group gathering in cities around the world, seeing how the graph reacts when I connect with people doing different things." Still intent on his readings, he chuckled, "You should have seen what happened in a gay bar."

"Should I have?"

"Oh yes. The readings were flatline dead," he said. "Because I personally shut down there, so nothing got through."

My radar was working, and I could feel the motion of my staff behind me. Maybe there was something to what the guy was saying: I could also feel their hostility toward me. I needed to get back to work.

"So, cottage cheese and milk. Anything else?"

"The two yang foods are fine," he said. "It'll be interesting."

I didn't ask what that meant. I wrote out a ticket for his order as I hurried to the kitchen to get it myself.

"Is he staying?" Thomasina called after me.

I nodded and didn't wait to hear her huff with

annoyance as I scooted down the corridor. The kitchen entrance was to the left, and the lavatory was to the right. My office was just beyond the restroom. I had the cordless phone in my apron pocket in case one of our regulars phoned ahead to have an order waiting. After Monday mornings, closing the door to that office was like a mini-vacation.

I went to the industrial refrigerator. The phone rang while I was there getting the cottage cheese. I didn't recognize the number; the prefix was a cell phone, and the name was May Wong. I took the call anyway, holding the phone between my ear and shoulder while I took out the tub o' cottage cheese.

"This is Murray's, Gwen Katz speaking."

"Hello. Do you cater?"

The voice was gentle, a little clipped, and male. Sure, sure, profiling is frowned on. But he sounded Asian.

"We absolutely cater, with little or no notice," I said enthusiastically, as I put the container on the worktable. "What are you looking for?"

"We are having a belt promotion at my school tomorrow night," the caller said. "There will be about twenty-five people."

"Piece of cake—or latke," I said. "What are you, a leather-working school?"

The only noise for the next second or so was me getting a soup spoon from a drawer. The other end was silent.

"I do not understand," the caller said. "This is

the Po Kung Fu Academy. I am Sifu Ken Chan. Our students are testing for their belt promotions."

Talk about missing by a mile. I got the voice all right but missed the heart of the matter. "Sorry. I'm from New York with relatives in the garment district. When you said 'belt'—"

"I understand. We each connect to our own shadows."

Oh, good. More esoterica. "We can do it," I said, getting back to something I knew—pastrami and cole slaw. "Can you call, or I can call you, after the breakfast rush so we can talk about exactly what you want?"

"I will stop by at ten-thirty, if that is all right. You are on the way to my school. A restaurant that is always busy must be a good one."

"Or cheap," I said.

"You are not so cheap," he replied. "I looked up your menu online."

"Touché, Mr. Chan. See you in a bit."

I finished ladling the cottage cheese into a soup bowl—I might as well give him a big portion for his yang—then poured his milk in a big beer mug. I wondered if his bones would expand right before my eyes.

Stop it, I told myself. *People used to think Jews had horns, too. Some still do. Don't judge.*

Still, it was difficult not to look at the man as a bit of an odd duck: he had his hands cupped on either side of the laptop, facing each other, moving very slightly as if he were sizing up one of my *tantas* for a bra. Just before I got there, he put his left hand in his lap. I set the bowl and mug on that side—where I'd intended to.

"Thank you very much," he said, without moving his eyes from the graph.

"Did you know where I was going to put them?" I couldn't help asking.

"Yes," he said. "They told me."

"*Aha.*"

He was unfazed by my obvious sarcasm. "All organic matter has a voice. It just depends on whether or not one chooses to hear it."

It was a gentle correction, not a put-down. He was nicer than I was.

"I'm Banko, by the way."

"Gwen," I said. "Is that your Christian name?"

He looked at me. "Buddhist."

"I meant—is that your first name, entire name . . . ?"

"My last name is Juarez. I was adopted by a Puerto Rican hotelier and his Danish wife. They were Catholic and Lutheran. I chose a different path."

"Clearly. Well, it was good to meet you." I tucked the new check under the first. "Enjoy your second course."

I had been negligent, my duties undone, as the hostile looks of Raylene and A.J. informed me. But part of my job was to make newcomers feel welcome, and except for the part about doubting that food could talk, that's what I was doing. Even though I *was* supposed to just get him out of there.

I behaved for the rest of the rush, hustling here and there as if the boss were watching. Which I was, I guess. I didn't even notice when Banko Juarez headed out, his dairy products untouched, his bills paid with a twenty and a five tucked under an unused spoon. The milk went back in the refrigerator for my cats. Banko did leave a nice tip, though, along with his business card, which I slipped in my apron pocket after glancing at it. I did not recognize the 305 prefix, and there was no address, just a website. I also had no idea what etheric cleansing was, but if it was anything like a high colonic, I did not want to know anything more about it.

I got to grab a mug of coffee, black, and closed my office door a little before ten. My mother used to say it was nice to sleep the sleep of the just at night after a long workday. After rushes, I sat the sitting of the just. My dad's old office chair was unsteady, and the vinyl was torn; the orange cushion had been crushed flat from the year I'd been sitting in it, but it was always a blissful place to plant my *tuchas*.

I'm not one of those people who social-networks, since I don't care what someone is doing or feeling at every given moment; if any of my friends from New York want my input, they call. There weren't many of those: no one had been down to visit since I came here. We're all busy, but New York people seem to be busiest when the alternative is to head to the South, even a city as culturally rich as Nashville. The attitude up there is pretty much that they have it all up there, unless it's in Europe. They will zip across the ocean.

I get e-mails from people I have generally superficial relationships with down here, like slumlord Stephen R. Hatfield, who has a kind of thuggish fascination with me and keeps suggesting we do this or that, attorney Dag Stoltenberg, who worked for my uncle and my dad and occasionally checks in, or Robert Reid, who publishes the *Nashville National* and still feels guilty about dating me without revealing his ulterior motive. Then there's Stacie, my almost half-sister, who worked for me a while before heading to Southern California with her fiancé. Through one of my old Wall Street connections, I got her a job as a teller in San Diego. She grew up poor and wanted to be around money. I couldn't blame her since, in my experience, being around money inspires you to want to make money. It's up to the integrity of the individual how that goes down. And of course I get a few messages each week from Detective Grant Daniels, my former inamorato, who had gone from liking me to hating me and was now somewhere in the middle. He sends links to articles he thinks might interest me even though they don't. Or they probably wouldn't if I bothered clicking on them. I send him polite responses, nothing more. I don't want anything more.

The e-mails I was looking for now were special deals from my vendors. These usually came early in the day, after the morning orders had been filled. Produce was especially volatile, and I could always make some kind of soup or potpie or even dried and seasoned chips with less-than-perfect veggies. It had been Dani's vegan-y idea to make and bag chips and overcharge for their healthfulness. It gave Newt something to prepare between rushes, and since we'd started two weeks ago we were doing okay with them from a spin-rack at Thom's post. I cut Dani in for ten percent of the net. I wondered what would happen when the waif was making as much from Katz Nips as she was working her butt off on the afternoon shift. The answer was not going to make me happy—but, once again, I get ahead of myself.

Thom thrust her head in to tell me I had a visitor, Ken Chan.

"I'll be right out," I said, grabbing the expanding folder where I kept menus and forms. We had those on our website but, like my uncle, I prefer to have hard copy to refer to. I finished my coffee and hustled out. The man standing beside the counter surprised me. He was about thirty-one or two, five-foot-three, bald, round-faced, and as thin as one of those ribbon-ties that come on a store-bought bag of bread. He wore jeans and a sweatshirt with sleeves cut off at the shoulder. His upper arms were bony, and both arms looked like noodles. He did not seem to be classically "in shape."

I offered my hand, and he accepted with the most tortured fingers I'd ever seen. They were knotted with tendons, turned this way and that from years of training, with nails that were longer than any I'd ever seen on a man.

"They're useful for grabbing an opponent or raking the eyes, eagle-claw style," he said, noticing my stare.

"Sorry for being so rude," I said.

"Curiosity is not rude."

"Thanks for that. I'm not from fighters. My only war wounds are cuts from the slicer and some stitches. How long have you been doing this?"

"Kung fu? Since I was three years old."

"Wow. I was still trying to master finger painting at that age."

"Did you master it?"

"Not really, but I had fun making a mess," I said. "Though, come to think of it, I started playing piano when I was five. It's like an artistic bat mitzvah. All young Jewish girls do it."

"Each culture has its way of addressing fine motor skills." He chuckled. "When I was young, about five or six, I started training for grabs and strikes by plunging my stiff hands into pails filled with sand, then pebbles, then rock," he said. "It makes them strong, but as you've noticed, the bones do not emerge unimpacted."

I looked him over. "You have, what, zero body fat too?"

"I have always been lean."

"You don't eat a lot of potato pancakes."

He smiled. "I eat vegetables and fruit, and occasionally fish," he said, eyeing one of the cellophane bags beside Thom.

"They're four ninety-five a bag," Thom said dryly, clearly put off by our conversation. She went into her sell spiel: "Zero fat. Zero cholesterol. Big taste."

Thom was not so svelte, and she mistrusted anyone who was thin. That came from her devout religious background, she said. Thom associated skinniness with asceticism and self-denial. That meant skinny people had something to atone for. That meant they were sinners. She said that big, beautiful people suffered from occasional gluttony but were otherwise happy enough not to sin in other ways. One could argue with that logic but not dislodge it.

I pulled a bag from the rack and gestured toward a corner table. "On the house. You can munch while we talk."

He thanked me with a nod as we made our way through the dining area. I stopped at the near-empty counter and did a double take: a man at the end was working on a laptop. For a moment, I thought crazy Banko had returned. Had that entire conversation really happened? It already seemed like a strange, murky dream. But there was part of me that had to admit being a tiny bit impressed: as my mother used to ask when I was dating a dot-com entrepreneur or a financial blogger, "He makes a living at this?" I often wondered what she would think of the likes of her friend Mr. Feld, who once ran a flea market but had moved from a corner parking lot on the weekend to proliferate on eBay.

I leaned toward the heat lamps. "Luke, would you bring an egg-free matzo ball, and a latke, gefilte fish, and horseradish sampler?"

"Is it Passover already?"

"Must be. You're plaguing me."

Luke made a face as I caught up with Chan. He held out my chair. That felt nice. He sat, placing his cell phone on the table and folding his hands in front of him.

Setting up the menu took all of five minutes. Chan told me most of his students were carnivores who would chow down after they'd been tested and their guests would eat everything else. So it was the typical deli meat, potato salad, cole slaw, pickles, latke, farfel menu. Luke arrived with the samples I thought we'd need just as Chan was handing me his credit card. I returned to the table after giving it to Thom, just he put down a toothpick that had been stuck in a section of latke.

"That was good," he said.

"Are you new to our cuisine?"

"Not at all."

"I haven't seen you here before."

"Do you remember everyone who eats here?"

"Only when they show up again," I told him truthfully. "Otherwise, who cares about them?"

He laughed. "I understand. I am new to the area, not to deli food. I used to live in New York City." He must have seen my face brighten because his did as well. "You too?"

"Born and raised and missing it. Where did you live?"

"On Mott Street, near Bayard."

"God, I *love* that area!"

"As did I," he said wistfully as he sampled half of a tomato pickle. "But there was an ugliness underneath."

"What kind? Drugs?"

"Worse," he said. "You know about the triads?"

"No. What are they?"

"They're a criminal element that thrived for decades in Hong Kong under British control," he said. "Their name comes from their use of triangle designs to mark their territory. These ruthless people have been driven from Hong Kong by the Chinese, and when they came to America, they moved into our neighborhood. They were not just selling drugs and trafficking in human beings, they were also hiring extortionists, kidnappers, and assassins to extend their influence. Young people were coming to our school for training to fight in gangs. I could not abide that. It is not the lesson I wish to teach."

"Understandable, and sad. How long have you been here?"

"Six months. You?"

"Fourteen months," I told him.

Thom arrived with the credit card slip, which he signed. She was miffed about the free bag of chips I'd given him. I ignored her.

"Why Nashville?" I asked him.

He smiled. "I love country music, especially Johnny Horton. 'In 1814 we took a little trip . . .'"

I joined in, and we sang a few more measures of "The Battle of New Orleans," which had also been a favorite of my uncle's, along with "Sink the Bismarck." I remember him playing them both on our Baldwin upright when I was a kid. I wasn't smiling from the memory or the song but from the joy in Chan's eyes.

"You go to any of the local clubs?" I asked.

"Often. I enjoy watching people move. That is how kung fu was developed—by watching nature in its untamed state. My forebears were not permitted to have weapons, so they defended themselves by learning from the mantis, the snake, the eagle, bamboo moving in the breeze."

"I like that," I said. "I always thought it was something the Japanese invented for World War Two."

"Their arts are judo and jujitsu," he said. "It came to these shores after the war. Soldiers brought it back, and a few schools were opened. Kung fu was a closely guarded secret until Bruce Lee brought it into the open."

"What's the difference between them—judo, karate, kung fu?"

"National styles have their own cultural character reflecting the nature of the people," he said. "The short answer is that Japanese forms are outward reaching. They are basically big, circular motions that use an adversary's attack against him. Kung fu comes from here," he touched his sternum with those sharp nails. "It rises from your own center, your own chi—your energy. It is very, very powerful. You can use it literally to push a person across a room with just your fingertips."

"That's something I could use here," I said. "You'd be surprised how many marriages, business relationships, and first-time novelists decide to go crazy over lunch." I noticed him looking at the matzo ball. "It's okay. There's no egg, no animal products. We use gluten as a binder."

"I am not a vegan. I would eat egg if not for the cholesterol."

He picked up the shrimp fork Luke had put on the plate, then did something deft with his fingers that turned the fork tiny ties-down. He poked it into the matzo ball and picked it up. He continued to look—at the matzo ball? I couldn't tell.

"Is something wrong?" I asked.

He was silent, suddenly contemplative. I looked more closely at him and noticed that he wasn't looking at the matzo ball but at the napkin holder directly behind it. The silver side of the freshly filled container showed a distorted reflection of what was behind me, outside the window in the busy street. I couldn't make anything out. Just as I turned to see what had gotten his attention, Ken Chan threw himself to the floor, an arm extended across my chest, taking me with him. The matzo ball flew skyward, the fork still in it, exploding when it hit the side of the counter—but not due to the impact.

It had been shot.

Chapter 2

It's a funny thing about chaos. It happens right away, surrounds you before you are even consciously aware of any danger. There's tumult, a rumbling, a darkening, or a noise—like the shot that sent the matzo ball flying—and then it's all around you, like a sewing needle that binds everyone with the same long thread.

I saw it in New York whenever a motorcycle would rev suddenly or a truck would cough or a car would swerve or a nutcase would scream in a small bodega or some homeless guy would suddenly decide to veer in your direction while you were walking the dog.

In this case, there was an object in motion and the loud crack of the gun. Both stimuli triggered the same sudden, purely physical fight-or-flight reaction in everyone around me. Everyone chose flight, and sensibly so.

As carefully as I could remember before panic partially wiped my brain, Chan had moved before the bullet even struck. He took me to the floor and lay on top of me, and that was why his back instead of my front took the rest of the gunfire. I could feel him pulse as each one hit, his thin frame twitching against me. Ironically, each was like a little heartbeat in different parts of his body.

I could hear screams from inside the deli, from the street, from my own throat. My cries had more of a whimpering quality as blood quickly pooled on the floor, warming and soaking my left side, and Ken Chan went from warm, breathing, and purposely protective to lifeless but still positioned between me and the fusillade.

The gunfire seemed to last for a week. I'm sure it wasn't more than five seconds. My first thought was that I didn't feel wounded or numb anywhere; my second thought was for my staff. I rolled my savior onto his back, his dead eyes staring up, as I kicked my heels back against the blood. I grabbed a chair to my right, got on it, looked around.

"Everyone! Answer me!"

It was stupid, but that's what came from my mouth. My hearing was heightened by the crack and crash of the glass. There was a flood of mixed, indecipherable, high-pitched cries, chairs scraping the floor, loud shouts, and horn honks through the broken window, so I looked around. I saw Thom rising from behind the register, which was untouched by the shooting.

Customers had crouched or dived for cover on the floor, but no one appeared hurt. A.J. was standing behind the counter, near the hallway, frozen in place with a tray of beverages. Raylene was just coming down the hall from the lavatory. Luke and Newt had been in the kitchen.

The attack had been localized on the table where we were sitting. The front window was shattered, and the street was empty, people evidently having bolted for cover.

I heard screaming. It was Thom, and she was stepping over customers and shoving aside chairs people had vacated to get to me. I saw her, saw she was looking at my chest with horror, saw that my apron and sleeves were soaked with blood.

"It's not mine," I said, hearing my own cottony voice, as though someone else was speaking. I patted my chest, sides. "I'm okay." Nothing hurt except my elbow, which had hit the tile floor.

"Lawsy," Thom said when she saw the body of Ken Chan.

I pulled off my apron, draped it over him. The bag of chips was beside him, torn open by a bullet, the particles floating in the widening puddle of blood turning from green and orange and yellow to red.

I heard sirens. I felt hands on me, Thom's hands, pulling me away from the body.

"Come to the office," she said.

"No." I backed against a stool, sat on it, leaned back against the counter. "I'm okay."

"You just survived a drive-by shooting."

That refocused my attention. "Is that what it was?"

"That's what it was. Just like when I was a little girl," Thom said. "Supremacists fired at us from their pickup while we worked our farm."

"Did you see them?"

"Only their tail end as they drove away," Thom said.

Luke brought me water. I ignored it. I told Thom to see to the others. I was vaguely aware of Raylene telling the few customers they should wait for the police to provide statements. I couldn't stop looking at the dead man. Whether by instinct or—more than likely, as I replayed the moment in my mind—by design, he had saved my life. I was overwhelmed as I realized how I had been avoiding men for the last few weeks, yet one had just shielded me, someone he barely knew. Maybe my perspective had gotten a little self-centered.

Speaking of which, by the time Detective Daniels arrived I—and the dead man—were the only ones left in the restaurant. The humming in my ears had dissipated, and every sound seemed super-sharp now, like digital. Especially the sound of footsteps on shattered window glass.

"Wait out here," I heard a voice say. I looked over as Grant walked in the door, which a uniformed NPD officer was holding open. Grant was a solid six-footer with broad shoulders and a square, determined jaw anchored by a strong, determined chin. His eyes found me at once. He seemed concerned and relieved at the same time.

He motioned for the rest of his team except for the medic to wait as he came over, carefully sidestepping anything in the immediate vicinity of the body. He stepped between me and the body, his back to me, as the doctor squatted, took the man's exposed wrist between his fingers—it was already a bluish white—and made sure he was dead. He laid it back down and shook his head. Grant motioned him off. He turned to me.

"Were you hit anywhere?"

"No."

"Any breaks, cuts—?"

"I'm all right. He protected me." I rolled my chin in the direction of the body.

"Who is he?"

"Ken Chan," I told him. "He has a martial arts school. New in town, just six months out of New York."

"I know the school," Grant said. He took me gently by the upper arm. "I'm going to get you to the ambulance, have them check you out."

That was probably a good idea, but my mouth didn't want to work at that moment. I nodded.

Police tape was already up, so the onlookers and picture takers and cell phone videographers were back a distance as I was walked out to the ambulance. I don't crave attention, and ordinarily the gawkers would have made me very uncom-

fortable. But I was alive. As I began to realize
how close I came to that no longer being the
case, the more I didn't care about the crowds—
and the more my heart began to drum and my
breath to speed up. Grant went back inside
when he had handed me over to an EMT. She
sat me on a gurney in the ambulance, which is
where it really hit me: the young woman had
barely gotten the band around my arm to take
my blood pressure when I started to panic.

"I need to get out," I said.

"Ma'am, we really need to make sure nothing's broken or—"

"No. I'm fine. I'm leaving."

In the past year I'd slipped on water, grease,
slices of tomato, and a pork chop. I'd taken
worse falls than this. Still, when I stood, it was un-
steadily. Her partner, who was a five-foot *petsl*,
put his hands on my shoulders to convince me
to sit back. I rolled my arms and shrugged him
off; he held up his hands in the universal "it's
your ass" sign and turned to enter the session in
a laptop on the medicine cabinet behind him.

I walked cautiously down the little fold-out
stepstool. The *tzimmes* inside didn't have to do
with the fall but with the event itself. As I reached
the sidewalk and turned to my left, I saw, for the
first time, my shot-up deli window. It was ugly,
unfamiliar, dead. I had a vision, probably from
my great-great relatives having talked about it,
of broken Jewish storefronts in Germany before
the war. I felt nauseous, something that didn't

happen often. Police were photographing the pavement, the asphalt, were walking around with tape measures that stretched from the window to imaginary points at the curb. That's the sad thing about urban police. They know the drill.

Back inside I saw Grant and his team surrounding the body, collecting evidence. The rest of the staff was in the kitchen talking to another detective, one I didn't know, a woman of color. I walked that way, not wanting to be around the body. The woman was talking to Newt by the back door, which was opened to the fenced-in area and dumpster. Luke and the rest of the waitstaff were standing behind the stainless-steel table where I'd scooped out the cottage cheese. They were huddled, round-shouldered and whispering, like Shakespearean conspirators. Thom was at the other end of the table, in front, leaning on one hand and clutching a napkin in the other. She was staring low, at nothing, while her mouth moved. In prayer, I was certain.

I walked over to her and touched the sleeve of her floral-pattern blouse. She grasped my hand without looking at me or stopping her silent prayer. She touched the napkin to her eyes. I hugged her arm lightly.

Newt came over and quietly informed me that the detective would like to talk to me. I nodded, squeezed Thom's hand—noticing now that my fingers were swollen and hurt—and went over to the open door. The woman's eyes were fresh, alert, sharp like those of one of my cats. She was about six-one and built like she belonged on a beach volleyball team. Her hair was straightened and pulled back in a very severe ponytail. She was probably in her early thirties but carried herself as though she was older, battle-hardened. I saw a long scar on the back of her right hand when she extended it.

"Detective Jill Bean," she said.

"Gwen Katz." She had a grip like giant pliers.

"Ms. Katz, I'm sorry to have to do this now, but we need to talk while the memory is still fresh."

"A half hour ago I was talking to a man who's dead now. That's pretty fresh."

"I understand, but sometimes there are details—"

"This event is like canned goods," I said. "It'll keep a very long time."

I hadn't intended to make a joke, but it sounded like one and it fell flat. Detective Bean gave me a mild if-you-say-so look before asking if I wanted to sit. I told her no. I leaned against the jamb with the smell of the kitchen to my right and sun-ripened trash to my left. It fit the situation. She turned on her iPad voice recorder and asked me to tell her what happened in as much detail as I could remember.

As my staff quieted, apparently listening to every syllable I uttered, I told the detective everything from the moment Ken Chan walked in until Grant walked me out. She did not interrupt.

When I was finished, she asked what I had seen when I looked out the window.

"I saw the tail end of a car, a motorcycle, and the front of another car," I told her. "There were flashes, like sunlight hitting the window, and then the room turned over as Mr. Chan threw me to the floor."

"Did the flashes originate in one of the vehicles or on the sidewalk?"

"It was from above the street, definitely not the sidewalk."

"How far above?"

"I think—about the height of a delivery truck."

"A rooftop, perhaps?" she asked.

"Maybe. Yes, probably."

"You're sure."

"There was a pedestrian—she looked across the street. Up, I think."

"So there was the tail end of a car, a motorcycle, the front of another car, *and* a pedestrian. They all may have seen the shot?"

"Yes," I said.

"What did this pedestrian look like?"

"A woman. Short. With a dog. She was dressed in jeans and a white blouse."

"Were there earbuds? Was she listening to music?"

"I don't know. Most likely. Everyone does."

"Okay. You're sure there was nothing else."

"Yes. Isn't there surveillance video?"

"We're checking," the detective said.

"You say Mr. Chan threw you . . ."

"It was more like he stuck his arm out and pushed me." I showed her, with my hands, how we were sitting at right angles to one another.

"He clotheslined you," she said. "It's like when you run into a clothesline you didn't see and it knocks you flat on your back."

"That's pretty much what happened," I agreed, "except that I wasn't moving before that. He provided all the force. His arm didn't look strong, but it was."

"Had you ever met Mr. Chan before today? Know anything about him?"

I shook my head. "The first contact I had was when he phoned this morning."

"He called first?"

"Yes."

"What showed up on your phone? What name?"

Good question. I had forgotten about that. "May Wong," I told her.

She wrote that down. "The number is still on your phone?"

I nodded.

"Did he say anything about his personal life?" she asked.

"He said he left New York because of pressure from gang members."

That got her attention. "Did he mention any affiliations?"

"He said something about the triads."

"You say he was ordering food for a belt test," she said. "When was that for?"

"Tomorrow night."

I choked on the words; I don't know why. It hit me behind the eyes, and I started to sob. The detective stepped back to give me space, and I turned away. I looked out at the clear, sharp sunlight smeared by my tears. Maybe I had just realized that this wasn't about me or even Ken Chan. What was supposed to be a happy time, a joyous place, would now be a scene of mourning. I wondered suddenly if I should cater whatever kind of memorial service they would have. Would that be a welcome gesture or in poor taste? I would have to find out.

"Was he married?" I asked.

"Yes, with a young daughter," the detective told me. "We have someone with them now."

"Those poor people."

"What about other impressions?" she asked. "Did he seem relaxed, attentive?"

"He sampled the food, wanted to be sure the menu would please his students and their guests, and—"

"What?" she asked as I hesitated.

I was replaying the moment in my head. Then it hit me. "No, he wasn't looking at the matzo ball. I thought he was, but he was looking just past it. At the napkin holder?"

The detective scrolled backward on the tablet, which was auto-transcribing what I told her. "You said he was looking at the matzo ball. Now you think it was the napkin holder?"

"I don't know. It didn't seem like he was seeing something, actually, but thinking something. I just don't know."

Still reading from the iPad, she said, "But you still say you had time to turn and look out the window. 'Like Governor Connelly in the Zapruder film,' you put it."

"That's right."

"Could he have seen something or someone *reflected* in the napkin holder? Something or someone he thought he recognized? A vehicle, a person, a weapon?"

"It's possible. He just froze there with a matzo ball on the end of a shrimp fork."

"And you're certain he didn't turn to the window?"

"Positive."

"Do you think he was afraid someone would recognize him?"

I thought for a moment. "I don't know. Why would he be afraid of that? We were sitting right in the open. He didn't sneak in."

"Just pursuing angles," the detective said. "Ms. Katz, this is a tough question, and I'm asking you to speculate. Impressions are important. Are you sure he pushed you, or could he have just struck you while he was getting out of the way?"

"He pushed me. That was my very, very strong feeling at that moment. Why does it matter?"

"Because it could be the difference between diving for cover in an unexpected situation or knowing he was out of time and wanting to avoid collateral damage. That will help me to sharpen the questions I ask Mrs. Chan, spare her a longer interview."

I nodded.

"Are you still as sure as you can be that he pushed you?"

"I am very, very, *very* sure. That arm came at my chest, level and precise. I've probably got a bruise. Mr. Chan could have shoved me to one side. But that would have exposed me to the track some of the bullets ended up going as the gun passed by outside. No, he got me totally out of the line of fire and then grabbed onto me to keep me there. He saved the life of someone he didn't even know."

Detective Bean smiled. "Thank you. That's helpful. One more question, and I need you to be really candid with me here. You can even be creative."

"Murder arts and crafts?" My mouth was moving, that was all.

Bean ignored the comment. "Is there anyone, Ms. Katz, who might have a grudge against *you*? Say, a customer you might have argued with today or last week? An angry former employee? A jealous significant other? I understand you inherited this place—were there other family members who might have wanted it?"

The question surprised me, along with the exceptionally wide reach of her net. I felt oddly naked and a little violated.

"Are you asking my staff the same question?"

"I'm doing a thorough homicide investigation," she replied. "Is there anyone we should talk to?"

She was clearly going to be a linebacker on this matter, so I ran through my mental yearbook. Was there anyone voted Most Likely to Kill Gwen—other than the people who had already tried in the course of my short but storied career as a private eye, a regular Jessica *Fleyshik*? I gave her a few names, adding that Grant already knew about them. She said she'd check them anyway. But I assured her they were nothing.

"Why?" she asked.

"Because none of them was NRA material, to my knowledge; their attacks on me were more or less crimes of passion, heat of the moment; most are in jail; and none of them has enough money or anything to trade to hire a hit man or woman."

She asked for the spellings, corrected them on the transcript, then reviewed what I had said.

"You didn't mention what time Mr. Chan first called," she said. "Do you remember when that was?"

"Height of the rush, between a quarter and half-past eight."

"Would it be possible for me to borrow the credit card receipts from that time until the attack?"

"Why?" I asked.

"Someone might have been casing the place, knowing that he'd be here," she said. "It's routine."

"But the credit card information—isn't that confidential?"

"I'm not going to buy a flatscreen TV or plane tickets on someone else's dime," she said. "I want to see if anyone who ate here this morning has a criminal record. I want to catch a murderer, and I'm sure you do too. I'll scan them to a file, then delete them when I'm done. They won't even have to leave the premises. But if you want to waste time while I get a subpoena—that's your call."

"No, it's okay," I said.

I wasn't a member of the ACLU, and given how I ran the place, I believed in a little benevolent dictatorship. And she was right. I asked Thom to gather the slips. Detective Bean thanked me. She ran them across a plug-in to her iPad as if they were items in a grocery checkout line.

"Oh, and I'm sorry," I said when she was done.

"About what?"

"My crack about the freshness of my memory. Apparently, you did need to prod me."

"People recall a lot but remember selectively," she said. "Trauma causes what we call the Disco Ball Effect. The bright spots shine, the details are sometimes lost." She gave me a card. "If you remember anything else."

"Sure."

I was left feeling stupid and empty. You always wonder how you'll respond if you're ever really tested by something horrible. I always imagined I'd keep my head, deal with the situation like Molly Pitcher ramrodding her Revolutionary

War cannon at the Battle of Monmouth. The truth is, even as the event rolled out in what seemed like slow motion, I didn't have time to do anything except turn my head. I didn't process the danger fast enough. Even falling, my arms barely had time to take the hit. I don't know what Ken Chan saw, but now that I thought about it, he obviously took that second or two to assess the threat, decided he was doomed, and made his move to save me.

Jesus.

My fingers were throbbing now, and I looked at my palms. They were black-and-blue from wrist to mid-thumb. So were the edges of my pinkies and all the tops of my fingers. But that, and some tightness in my shoulders, was all I got. I wondered when survivor's guilt would hit me. That was another bequest from my great-great relatives.

I went to my office, looked down the hall, and saw local WSMV Channel 4 TV reporter Candy Sommerton shooting video over the crime-scene tape, past the cop at the door, right at me. If poor Mr. Chan hadn't been lying on the floor a few feet away I would have flipped her out. That seemed disrespectful, under the circumstances. I just turned, entered my office, and shut the door.

Chapter 3

Crime is like a loose tooth. When it's in your face, you can't stop playing with it.

Grant kindly stopped by the office to see how I was, showing old-Grant concern for me. I was touched without being moved. In my defense, I was busy calling my insurance agent and various contractors and glaziers. If the past was any indication, business would boom due to what had happened. That wasn't why I made the moves to get repairs on the calendar; my staff needed to work, and so did I.

The calls were all rote. They took about a half hour, after which I went back to the kitchen. Detective Bean was talking with Thom. As I looked down the corridor I saw the body of Ken Chan being wheeled out under a white sheet. There was very little blood. Most of that was probably on my floor.

Grant was following the body out. He looked back, saw me, came over.

"We'll keep the tape up and two officers to move the rubberneckers along," he said. "I can recommend a good cleanup crew if—"

"I'll do it," I said.

"Gwen—"

I held up my hand to stop him. I saw the blood on my sleeve. "If I don't do it myself, it's always going to be there like a snapshot."

He looked at me sadly. "I understand. Anything I can do?"

"Yes. When you talk to his family, please tell them I'm sorry."

"Sure," he told me.

I knew him well enough to know, from that tone, that he wouldn't be mentioning my name anywhere near them. That was okay. I'd do it myself. They had to know what their husband and father did for me.

Detective Bean followed Grant by a few minutes, after which I marshaled the troops in the kitchen. There was no door—swinging doors are just as dangerous as they appear in the Three Stooges—so we moved to the enclosed pantry. Though open, it was out of view of the dining room and Candy Sommerton and the flashing of cameras in the street. There, among the shelves of canned goods and bags of flour, sugar, and other perishables, we were like a little family in a bunker.

That was when we all lost it. We hugged, huddled, clutched, and said nothing. It may only have been a minute; I don't know. But we all felt cleansed somewhat when we were through.

"We're glad you're okay," A.J. said, as she blew her nose with a handkerchief from her apron.

"Did anyone call Dani?" I asked.

"She called me," Luke said. "She wanted to come down—I told her not to. I said I'd come and see her as soon as the police were done."

"Good idea," I said. "Okay, look. I want you all to go home. I'm going to stay and clean up—"

"Not alone you ain't," Thom said.

"Alone I am," I insisted. "You are all going to march out the door and not look to your right. There are reporters out there, and if you want to talk to them, it's your call. Just remember that if you go down that road and you lose it, you're a viral video. So I suggest you just keep your eyes down and your mouths shut and let the police help you through if necessary. If anyone doesn't feel like driving, we'll call a cab."

"I'll drive whoever doesn't want to," Newt said.

"Thanks," I said. "I've called to get the place fixed up over the next few days, and obviously there won't be any eat-in. But I still want to open the kitchen for takeout."

"People will think we're cashing in on the shooting," Raylene said.

"People are pathetic gossips," I told her. "If we don't open they'll say, 'I hear they're closing,' even if they haven't heard that."

"They do like the sound of their voices," Thom said.

"Exactly. So we do that starting tomorrow. I'll be outside with menus, explaining the situation to anyone who asks and dealing with anyone who thinks it's in bad taste."

A.J.'s mouth twisted. "I was actually wondering that. Isn't it?"

I looked at her. "How do you honor a man who did what that stranger did? By putting your life on hold or moving ahead?"

"I would say a little of both," she replied. "Maybe put up a sign that says we'll be open for table service on Friday and not advertise that we are open for takeout."

My instinct was to tell her no. But I needed my staff to be on board. It could be that they needed a day off. I looked at Newt, then Luke, then Thom. "I had planned to bring everyone in— but you three are the ones I'd need most. What do you want to do?"

Thom answered first. "I just want to go to church and get on my knees and stay and thank God for your life and pray for the soul of the man who gave his. But I can do that tonight and be here tomorrow."

I looked at Luke. "I kinda want to be with Dani, and I think she wants to be with me. But I'll do what you say, boss."

Newt shrugged and said, "Whatever works for you."

I did not rule over a democracy. But I'd asked, and the staff had answered. "All right," I said. "Tomorrow it is." I looked at A.J. "But I appreciate that you told me your concerns."

She smiled weakly. A.J. and Raylene liked me, I think. But, older by a score of years than the kitchen crew and waitstaff, they looked out for the kids in the trenches. Because Thom looked out for me, they waged the proxy wars so we didn't have to fight. If this wasn't a first, it was a rarity.

I hugged everyone individually, then told them to go. Luke considered going out the back door and climbing the fence, but I vetoed that. I told him that if the cops saw him, they might think he was a finger man for the shooter, hiding out there.

As they left, I thought about the credit card receipts and wondered if there *had* been someone here. It seemed absurd: you wouldn't need to case a place you were going to shoot up from the outside. At least, I couldn't think of a reason. Unless they figured I might take him to the office. It would be easy to get a peek inside when someone went to the loo.

And then do what with that information? I wondered.

Could be that someone signaled the car that we were sitting in the dining room and it was okay to pull the trigger. Literally.

I shut my brain down as I went to clean up the

blood. The cops outside saw me bring out the mop and bucket and made sure that even the people on the outside of the tape moved along. That included Candy and her camera operator. My nemesis protested, and her videographer tried to get a shot of the bucket, but I went over, shut the door, and pulled down the shade. There was still the jagged hole that had been ripped through the center of the window, destroying most of "Murray's." But the blocked-off sidewalk and moving traffic made it impossible for anyone to linger. Why they would want to do that was a puzzle. I used to think that rubbernecking was an atavistic bloodlust, but those same people would look away from a squirrel or deer that had been hit on the highway or a bird that had flown into a window and snapped its neck. Maybe it was a secret dislike for humankind. Or a there-but-for-the-grace-of-God reaction. I didn't know, other than that I never had it.

I turned off the overhead lights and moved the tables and chairs back, creating an arena-like feel to the big oval of blood. I stared at it, transfixed. The blood was deep, oxygenated red in the daylight, with a syrupy consistency. There were streaks and smears, almost like strong brushstrokes, where the body had been moved or dragged. There were no footprints. The awful canvas was pure Ken Chan, save for the part on the top, near the counter. That was my collaboration, a diaphanous, wing-like shape where my arm and hip had been.

Part of me—a part I honestly didn't recognize—wanted to preserve it as a memorial, rope it off like at a museum. Another part of me—also from Gwen Terra Incognita—started examining it like an ink blot. But it was asymmetrical, so I didn't see any images. I thought of clouds, wondered if there was some kind of shape, a message from beyond.

All of that flashed through my head in a moment. It lasted about as long as it took to sigh tremulously, suck down another breath, then push the mop across the oval of blood. I began to clean before the horror in my heart rose up and challenged my resolve. I told myself to keep going, that life was marked by the ripples it caused and not the fluids that drove the engine. This wasn't the man who had saved me. He was gone.

I moved quickly, then urgently, then almost frantically. The blood was now just a messy film on the floor, dirty water in a pail. There weren't even any nicks in the floor from bullets. Ken Chan's slender body had absorbed them all. I worked by rote as I relieved the moment when I had been in *that chair,* the one just ahead of me. I suddenly savored the thumping of my heart, the anxiety in my belly, the air in my throat—being alive. And as the blood vanished and that seconds-long eternity stopped replaying, when every pop of a closing trunk or bang of a rolling delivery truck door returned to being just background noise, not gunfire, my brain went somewhere else.

I had been going back and forth about visiting the martial arts school Chan had founded, about meeting the family he left behind. If not for me, he might still be alive. I didn't know if I wanted to subject myself to those looks, that raw sadness or hate. But as I swabbed the tile and wrung the man's blood into a bucket, I decided I had to go. I needed those ripples of his life to permanently wash away the blood at my feet.

Chapter 4

The last thing I needed was another visitor.

I had just been outside in the fenced-in area out back, at the drain in the center of the asphalt. Pouring the contents of the bucket down a storm drain seemed more fitting than spilling it down the sink. For one thing, I wasn't sure I could lift the filled bucket. More important, it was closer to the earth, more like a burial. So that's where Mr. Chan went.

The task was a little lighter by then. Under the early afternoon sun, I found myself remembering his expressions as he sat at the table. It was strange how I'd cycled through the entire mourning process in about a half hour.

By two PM a truck had arrived from Umberto Professional Repairs. Like so many people down here, Umberto Delmonico and his son Vittorio had been friends of my Uncle Murray.

"He fed me on days when I went solo and

couldn't pay him," the older man said. "I'm glad I can be here for his niece."

I had heard that before from people, but under the circumstances, it propped me up no less than he did with the big piece of plywood in my front window frame. Umberto and his rugged young son braced it with a thin steel crossbeam on the inside.

"Nothing's getting through that," Umberto said when they were finished. Then he threw a muscular hand around him. "Don't let the darkness get you down. It will pass."

I tried to hold on to that as I put the furniture back in place, though the arrival of Lawrence Bowe-Pitt changed that.

I was in my office, answering e-mails from friends who had learned about the attack on the news. I heard the front door open and rolled my chair into the hall. A hulking white man stood just inside. He looked like the Michelin Man. He flipped out a little leather cardholder. There was a badge on top; he moved it to catch the light so I could see it from where I sat.

"Good afternoon. I'm Resident Agent Lawrence Bowe-Pitt of the FBI field office in Nashville," he said. "Are you Ms. Katz?"

"Yes."

"May I speak with you?"

I didn't bother pointing out that he already was. "Sure."

He had a voice like butter melting in the southern sun. Dressed in a charcoal-gray suit and thin black tie, the man mountain made his way toward me. I knew we'd never fit comfortably in the office—if he fit at all—so I went back into the kitchen.

I once met Bill Bradley, the former New York Knicks forward and senator, who ended up with an investment banking firm. Bradley stood six-five and seemed very, very tall. This man was about the same size but seemed even bigger than that because he had shoulders like an ox and a head that seemed a little too small for his massive frame.

I wasn't staring, but as he neared there was hardly a place you could turn where he wasn't. I had kept the coffee on and offered him a cup.

"No thank you," he said, in a voice that seemed to echo within that cavernous form, rolling around a few times before emerging from his thin-lipped mouth.

I went behind the counter and got some for myself. He followed me out.

"Don't you people usually travel in pairs?" I asked.

"Budget reductions do not always make that possible," he said. "And this is not, strictly speaking, an investigative visit."

"No? What is it?" I asked. I poured, sipped the coffee bitter and black, stayed where I was, and looked back at him. I wanted to be where the cop at the door could see me. I didn't know why, but I did.

He came around the counter, his back to the

door. There was no way the cop could see me now. If this guy wasn't the real deal, I was in serious trouble. I had no reason to believe he was a fake other than my own post-traumatic jitters, inherent mistrust, and doubt that this man could have worn even the extra-largest standard-issue FBI gear.

"We have been keeping an eye on all of the businesses like yours in Nashville," Agent Bowe-Pitt went on. "Nothing intrusive—just drive-bys several times a week."

"Why is that?" I asked, though I pretty much knew what he was going to say. "Like yours" was about as transparent a euphemism as one could use. He meant that some mouth-breather out there had it in for Jews.

"While it's possible that someone knew Mr. Chan would be here, that's a little too fluid a situation for me."

"I don't follow."

"Someone would have to have been tracking him," the agent said. "Given how often he was probably alone at his school, tailing him here doesn't seem to make the best sense. It's not impossible, of course, and there *are* some stupid killers out there, but it's not the best working theory."

"What is your best theory?"

"We've been tracking a well-funded group of radical white supremacists, the SSS," he said. "It stands for Shock, Shoot, and Slaughter. Mr. Chan, being of Asian descent, a foreigner, new in the city—that would have been something to attract their attention."

My first reaction? I didn't think that a bunch of homicidal rednecks would have had the wit or creativity to conceive of a mash-up between the SS and the KKK. Maybe they had hired an image consultant. I couldn't help but wonder if there was an opportunity there—rebranding hate. Legitimizing the illegitimate, the way nations did.

"You heard about the cop who was shot off-road two weeks ago?" he asked.

I nodded. It was big news for several days. Marcuz Frank, an off-duty police officer, had taken his date to a romantic spot off Briley Parkway. It wasn't really romantic; it was isolated and located in a woody depression not visible from the road. The gal was abducted, and the cop was fatally shot in the head. She was found later, strangled, in a rusting, abandoned truck.

"We believe that was the work of this group," he said. "The officer was African-American. The woman was not. The first flyers were found the next morning, not far from there."

"Had the couple been seen around town?" I asked. "How did they know?"

"We don't know," Bowe-Pitt said.

"I assume you know who these people are?" I asked. "Some of them, at least?"

"We don't," Bowe-Pitt admitted.

"Then how do you know they're well-financed?"

I asked. "A bunch of fliers pinned to trees isn't exactly high overhead."

"No, but invisibility is," he said. "These guys leave no data fingerprints anywhere. Either there are no cell phone or Internet communications, which isn't likely, or they are using highly sophisticated hardware and software. That costs."

True enough. It wouldn't be possible for a bunch of killer hillbillies to hide for very long without help.

"They've also been schooled in up-to-date security practices," he went on. "We have a flyer they posted. None of the word groups or letter sequences show up in any of our searches. And we don't know that they're remote country inhabitants, which I presume is what you meant by the hillbilly reference. For all we know they may be local business owners. Restaurateurs, perhaps."

Well, he sure put me in my place—making a point of using the slightly French-inflected word *restaurateurs*. Maybe I deserved it. I probably seemed like a snotty intellectual feminist to him, which I sort of was.

"What about the money? Any idea where it's coming from?" I asked.

"Cash doesn't leave a paper trail," he said. "You know the local economy. We're looking into businesses where cash can be skimmed."

There was a thoughtful silence, and I flinched as he slid a beefy paw into his jacket. I was prepared to hurl hot coffee in his face. But he didn't produce a shiv or garrote. He was holding a five-by-seven photograph of a flyer. He handed it to me. The original document was yellow and pinned to a tree. It said in a bold inkjet typeface:

THE U.S. IS FOR *US*
ARYANS ONLY
R VOICES WILL BE HERD
SHOCK SHOOT SLAWTER

"I assume the typos are mistakes," I said.

He looked at me as if to ask "What typos?"

"I mean, unless it's a creative flourish," I added quickly, turning the photo so he could see and pointing. "'Heard' as in audio, 'herd' as in a bunch of cattle. It could be a metaphor. And maybe 'slawter' is a service mark. I know. You can use it in commerce and see who sues. Then you've got them."

He continued to stare with practiced patience. I didn't imagine he met very many normal or well-composed people during his investigations: either they were bad guys or victims. I was anxious and babbling, but I couldn't help myself. As much as you hear about people hating, as much as your relatives pounded it into your skull, it's different when it's in your backyard—and potentially in your storefront. It turns your knees and bowels to water. You just want to run. Or flow, whichever gets you away best under the radar.

"I sincerely do not know about any of that,"

Bowe-Pitt remarked. "We found eleven of these flyers two weeks ago—"

"Eleven? Isn't that the number of states in the Confederacy?"

"It's also the number of trees located in Hadley Park, out of view of security cameras," Bowe-Pitt told me.

Okay, I thought. *I will say nothing more.*

"We have no leads on who might have put those up, other than a strand of thread that was attached to one of the nailheads," he went on. "We believe it's from a workman's glove, cotton with a trace of plastic coating. Electrical worker, perhaps. We're looking into it."

"That's a pretty impressive deduction from a piece of thread."

"We have a real good lab in Memphis," he said. "Of course, it could also mean a Nashville Electric worker pulled over to relieve himself and happened to lean on the tree. We're looking at gloves from workers on this afternoon's assignment sheet as well."

"You ought to wear gloves while you check *those* gloves," I said.

The agent ignored my quip.

"I checked with the NPD," he went on. "They will be leaving an officer posted outside tonight. I suggest, if it's possible, that you sleep here. Your home property is invasible."

My home property is invasible? What the hell kind of inflated thought process came up with that? Probably the same linguistic moron who told weather forecasters to refer to the afternoon as "afternoon hours" and humidity as "humidity values," as well as turning signs to "signage" and minutes to "minutage" and other idiotic neologisms.

Now I was babbling inside instead of out. I shut my brain up and listened.

"All right," I said.

"None of this is to say that we know for certain you were the target," he went on.

That's what "knowing" is, I mentally corrected him. Being "certain." I told my mind, again, to put a ball-gag in it.

He plucked a business card from that little leather wallet, which seemed lost in his fleshy hand. He laid it on the counter, beside the photograph of the flyer, and gave it two taps of his finger. He probably would have handed it to me if I weren't standing so far back that I burned my *tuchas* twice on the coffee machine.

"Call if you need me or if you hear or see anything," he told me.

"This hasn't exactly been reassuring," I told him.

"Sorry. We deal with information. Those are the facts and the suppositions."

"Fine. But before you go and before I stay, do you have any reason to *suspect* that my home may be a target?"

"We have to assume it may be."

There were enough qualifiers in that to make me feel like I was talking to the Duchess of Wonderland. "What I mean is, I have to go back and get my cats, some clothes, and I'd like to take a shower. That should be safe enough, right? In and out?"

He considered that. "I was planning to go out and have a look around your neighborhood, at the neighbors," he said. "If you can leave now—"

So the answer was *no,* it's not safe. I took another slug of coffee. "Let me just get my keys. You can follow me."

"I'll go on ahead," he said. "I'd like to be in the area when you get there."

"All right," I said.

He nodded a good-bye, then left. Watching him was like watching a low, solid storm cloud move across the city. The door opened and shut quietly, letting in a flash of sunshine that was like lightning. Then I was alone in the dark, dealing with the fear that had suddenly replaced my sorrow. With that feeling came a renewed sense of *What the hell am I doing down here?* I loved my staff, but they were culturally foreign to me and still employees. I enjoyed my customers, but they didn't know pastrami from corned beef. Ex-pats? Whenever I met them, I clung like they were the Messiah. That should tell me something. I didn't belong. I didn't want to be here. I *shouldn't* be here. I wasn't having fun.

You aren't beholden to anyone, I reminded myself. *Why don't you sell the place and leave?* But I knew the answer even as I asked the question. *Because you don't really have anywhere to go, anything or anyone to go to.*

I looked at Agent Bowe-Pitt's card. It listed a landline, a fax, and his cell phone under his name. It seemed official. If he was trying to lure me to my house to kill me, he'd gone to a lot of trouble. Especially when he could have just busted into my "invasible" home.

I decided that this was not the time to make impulsive decisions. Instead, I would take the time to figure out which of my *bubbe* Jennie's grandmotherly sayings applied: *A shlekhter sholem iz beser vi a guter krig* or *Kolzman es rirt zich an aiver, klert men nit fun kaiver.*

A bad peace is better than a good war or *As long as one limb stirs, one does not think of the grave.*

I put Bowe-Pitt's business card on my desk, beside that of Banko Juarez, then I took a turn around my wounded but cleaned-up deli. The air was heavy with Lysol. Except for that, without the staff, without the customers, without the daylight or the city intruding, the deli was very much me. It was my hard work that made it grow from just above break-even to solid profitability. It was my personality in the design of the menu, the place mats, the local paint-by-number flea market paintings on the walls, the improvements and changes and decorations I had brought to it over the past fourteen months.

I glanced down at the photograph, at the words, at the arrogant hate. And a third phrase came to my intellectual New York feminist Jewish brain.

Shtuppes.

Shove it.

Chapter 5

My home was a forty-year-old colonial that my late father and his brother had shared on the brilliantly named Bonerwood Drive. I shared it with the cats, some of my New York furniture, and, I'm told, a clutch of African-American Civil War laborers who were interred somewhere beneath the cellar. I wondered what Banko Juarez would make of them. I'd already tried witches, and you may recall how that turned out.

The mutty cats were transplants from New York. They were my loyal friends and companions during the acrimonious divorce from Phil Silver, now referred to in my brain as the Bitter Phil, Tarnished Silver, PS I Hate You, and any number of clever epithets. The mind games were a way to redirect my hate for that self-obsessed, argumentative mama's boy who adored me for about five seconds of our four years together. And those scarce little ticks of the clock were all frontloaded, so there were no oases during the eternity that followed. So why, you ask, did I stick with him? Why does anyone do that, except for all the wrong, fearful reasons? I was worried about hurting my mother, about losing our mutual friends and business associates, of feeling like a major flopola—in other words, every reason that had nothing to do with my actually being happy.

Southpaw and Mr. Wiggles were named for two of the happier times in my life: making it onto an all-boys little league team, simultaneously breaking the glass ceiling and a pitcher's hand with an angry line drive; and getting an A+ for a sixth-grade science project in which I managed to get worms to reproduce. That was in response to a stupid boy, Marius Hampton, who was convinced that they replicated by being cut in half.

The fact that my cats greeted me at the door told me that there was no one lurking in or around the home. When danger threatened the cats took a powder. I had no problem with that. Declawed cats would be of no use to me during a home invasion.

I showered. That was the first order of business, to wash away the antiseptic smell and whatever blood had splattered on my skin and hair. I didn't bother to dry my hair; the gentle coolness of the water against my scalp would help keep my brain from boiling. Then I got the two carrying cases, which would have sent the cats running—it usually meant a trip to the vet—if I hadn't taken the precaution of first taking them into the bathroom. Not a lot of room to run. I showered while I was there then—leaving the door open and an ear turned to it—then threw together an overnight bag. There was an air mattress in the garage, a holdover from when my father first crashed here, and I took that, along with a quilt and pillow. I didn't see Agent Bowe-Pitt when I went to the car, but I guess that was the point.

It was late afternoon when I got back to the deli. The tape was down, and there were no longer any crowds. I pulled up in front to off-load my stuff and had to show an ID to the new officer who had just come on duty. I parked in my usual spot in the public garage. I paid for parking, but not for the choice spot near the up-ramp. It was the old barter system: in exchange for dog bones at the end of the day, the attendant, Randy, always held it for me with a pair of orange traffic cones. I rounded the corner and walked past the Arcade, which was lined with cafés, shops, and salons. I sometimes snuck off for a late dinner here: as the Bible probably says somewhere, know thy enemy. The proprietors, who had seen me earlier, had hurried over to make sure I was okay. I know they were sincere. We fight it out with discount coupons and specials, but when one of our own is ailing we help them. When Adorf's Tacos was flooded and the electricity shorted, I let them bake shells in my oven. Seeing me now as

I hurried past, "Grandma" Marie, as everyone called the owner, ran out and offered to lend me a bicycle delivery boy if I wanted to reopen. I thanked her and told her I would definitely keep that in mind for tomorrow.

"I have more boys than I need," said the Vera Cruz–born woman, clasping a hand on my wrist. She gestured toward her restaurant. "I do not know how to do what you do, so lean. You know how to run a business."

What I heard, of course, is *"You people know how to run a business . . ."* Sometimes we hear things that aren't there. Sometimes people say things they don't realize. And sometimes we hear exactly what is being left unsaid.

I smiled and walked on, huffing inside at our lopsided society. If I'd said to her innocently, after the lunch rush, *"You look tired, you should take a nap,"* the ACLU or some do-gooder group would come after me for hate speech. *"You were saying that this Mexican-American should take a siesta. That's a destructive racial stereotype . . ."* There would be pickets and my business would be over, finished. *But shoot up a Jewish business . . . ?*

I told myself to slow down. We didn't know that was what had happened. My paranoia and genetically suspicious nature, passed down from the shtetls in the Ukraine, was telling me that.

I let the cats out in my office and closed the door. I checked the cash register. I couldn't use the alarm system because of the busted window. Thom had put the money in the safe in the back—artfully hidden behind bags of flour—and I didn't think anyone would climb the fence to get at my collection of Ginsu knives. I felt okay leaving the back door open so the cats would get some air.

I had the address of Chan's school from the form he'd filled out. I wasn't sure what I'd do when I got there, but I knew I had to pay my respects—even if that meant just passing by and laying eyes on the place. The address was about a half mile away on 4th Street S; I'd been inside long enough, immersed in the scent of death, and decided to walk. I set out after pulling my New York Yankees baseball cap low. Even with that brilliant disguise, a few nearby customers recognized me. They said my name and either nodded with sad little eyes or gave me one of those tense, terse hands up/hands down waves like they were greeting the Fuhrer. A few said vaguely that they were sorry. It was as though people weren't sure what they were feeling or how to express it. I filled in the blanks.

"Hi, Gwen. Or should I say Grim Reaper?"

"'Nashville' Katz? That's where you get Russian dressing and Russian roulette."

The sick thing was, the more people who dined and died on our watch, the busier we got. If I ever did decide to sell the place, I'd probably have to agree to stay for a year, just to make sure the body count increased. Call it the Angel of Death clause in my contract.

I had never been to a martial arts school. I

had never even seen a Bruce Lee or Jackie Chan film. I caught *Crouching Tiger, Hidden Dragon* on an airplane and fell asleep when people started flying. This was not my world. I stopped across the street and stared. The big window had "Po Kung Fu Academy" painted in yellow block letters, in the shape of a rainbow, across the middle. Beyond it was a single, shadowy room that was considerably longer than it was wide. There were floor-to-ceiling mirrors all along the left side. Blue vinyl mats filled most of the floor. There was an office in the back on the right side and what looked like a dressing room to the left. Between them were rows of folding chairs. Ordinarily they were probably filled with parents who had brought their kids to class. Today they were empty—though the school was not. There appeared to be people in the shadows in back.

I crossed the street against the light—an old New York habit that refused to die in more cautious Nashville—and approached the single-story, red-brick building. It was a quiet, calm location. Pedestrian traffic was extremely thin here. There was a parking area to the left and the corner of Elm Street to the right. A squad car was parked on the street. One of the officers got out as I approached. An Asian-looking woman, she stood beside the car but made no move to intercept me.

As I slowly approached the window, I could see my own distorted reflection layered over the interior. My eyes were drawn to a card table set against the mirrors. A framed photograph of Ken Chan had been placed in the center. Incense sticks burned in front of it. The tiny shrine was encircled by a frayed, slightly faded black belt. His belt, no doubt. With my face nearly against the glass I could clearly see four people standing in the shadows outside the office: three men, one small older woman.

I was surprised there weren't more people here. By now, word must have spread among the community. I remember the day our rabbi died. I was only seven years old, but the memory was vivid of throngs coming and going from the shul on 12th Street near University Place. Some people were wailing, some were sobbing, most were Jewish, many were not. The seats were never empty, and the davening, the prayers, flowed one into the other among a core of mourners as people stayed and talked and reminisced and probably plotted to make sure his replacement was more conservative or more reform or just the same.

My heart was thudding against my ribs, front and side. *Are you going in or not?*

If I did, what would I say? *"Hi, I'm Gwen. This wasn't my fault, right?"*

Someone inside saw me. A woman. She didn't move, but it was time that I did. I went to the door, and, after hesitating, rapped gently on the glass. I didn't know what the customs were and felt I should be invited in. Maybe this was alone time for the family.

The woman came over with ethereally light steps. She was just a little over five feet, maybe an inch or two, round of face and figure, and dressed in black slacks and a long-sleeved black top with white knot buttons: on one side was a knot, on the other a fabric loop. She turned a key on the inside of the door and pushed it open slightly. She looked up at me with tight lips, waited for me to speak.

I started, stopped. I looked into a face that resembled Chan's—a relative, I was sure—and felt the tears push at my eyes.

"I am Gwen," I said.

"You were with my nephew," she said. "The police—said the woman's name was Gwen."

I nodded. I had intended to say "yes," but the word snagged in my throat.

The woman continued to study me. "Sifu's wife is at home with their child. His mother is with them. My sons and I are making funeral arrangements and telephone calls. We will be receiving mourners at eight PM and again tomorrow evening."

Heads turned toward me and then away. I had not expected a welcome, but I don't think I was prepared for the hostility I saw in those faces.

"I wanted to say I was sorry—to someone," I told her.

"For what?"

"For being alive," I said.

She looked up at me with sadness that was fringed with compassion and maybe a few threads of caution that most cultures had for the intrusion of an outsider. I grabbed onto the compassion.

She was silent for a moment. "Please come back tonight."

"I'm sorry, I didn't want to intrude, but I had to see where he taught . . ."

"That was very thoughtful."

She waited expectantly. Either she was very perceptive, or I was disgustingly obvious. Possibly both.

"There is one thing, though," I said. "Did the sifu have enemies, an individual or a group who would do this to him? That's a terrible question to ask now, but he told me there were gang members in New York—I need to know which of us was the target."

The woman's expression changed, subtly. That little halo of compassion was swallowed entirely by sadness. "I don't have an answer to that. My sons spoke with the police, told them what they know. Come tonight. You may ask them."

"Tonight," I said. "I'm not sure."

Reluctant as I was to come back, I did need to know more. I looked in again. Presumably the time to ask was not now. The young men were all looking over, presumably to see if their mother was all right.

"I'll be here," I assured her. "Though I'm not sure it's a great idea."

Her face was like a strangely changing mask. There was a hint of a smile now. "You will not be unwelcome. That is not the way of kung fu."

Okay, I *did* see *Kung Fu Panda*, in which—spoiler alert—the secret ingredient to something or other was "nothing," and I did feel, just then, that I'd slipped into that cartoon. I remembered someone once saying that being with my family was like being in *Fiddler on the Roof.* Maybe we should all come tattooed with movie references, like bar codes, so people would know what to expect. Maybe the NPD could keep an eye out for the *Birth of a Nation* crowd.

The woman started to turn away.

"Is there something I should bring?" I blurted. "I mean, what is traditional?"

The smile broadened very slightly. "Bring what you carry."

That didn't help, but I smiled politely in response—directly at her, not at the turning heads in back. It wasn't my intention to snub them but rather not to be discouraged by them. The looks had not made me feel welcome.

As I crossed the street I noticed that the officer had come to the corner to watch what was going on. She was busy texting. She didn't seem too concerned . . . unless she was texting something about me.

I checked my cell phone messages as I walked back. There were calls from every member of the staff, all saying the same thing: we hope you've gone home by now. I texted them all that I was fine and I was walking around. I told them I was going to take it easy that night and that I would see them in the morning to hand out menus and deal with our takeout business. Thom still seemed to feel a little ghoulish about that. I cared, but not for my sake. I needed to work.

There was also a message from Grant, checking in and letting me know that the security cameras on my street had done nothing for them.

"The gunshots did not come from a passing vehicle or pedestrian," he said. "I'm disappointed we didn't get a lead, but not surprised. The angle was a little steep for that. We're looking at one of the rooftops across the street."

Terrific, I thought. Someone was waiting for the morning crowd to thin so they could get a clear shot at Chan or me. Inside, where we couldn't run.

Grant went on. "The good news, if there is any, is that there may have been a run through. A competitive marksman likes to reverse-engineer a target, if possible. Stand in front of the bull's-eye and look back—gauge refraction of the glass, glare, obstructions, that sort of thing. So your shooter may have been among the customers this morning."

That was good news if the customer had charged a meal. And owned a gun legally. And didn't have someone who would lie to give him an alibi. A friend in New York was one of the Manhattan assistant DAs. It was alarming how often a perfect storm of evidence was needed to get grand juries to sign on the dotted line. And that was New York. In Nashville, where cousins or neighbors were often the alleged perps, Grant once told me that the task was even tougher.

When I got back to the deli, I made an early dinner to compensate for skipping lunch. I did not return the call from Candy Sommerton or Robert Reid of the *Nashville National* or anyone else who wanted an interview. The sun set on me playing solitaire on the computer and feeling very, very trapped. The office felt darker than it was, street sounds—never dramatic, not like in New York—being muted by the big wall of plywood and steel up front. I had closed the back door so the cats now had to stay cooped up. The strong smell of the disinfectant I'd used on the floor added to the choking claustrophobia.

I got up suddenly, as though I'd decided something. I hadn't. It was just caged-tiger impatience. I stepped into the hall, failed to find any satisfaction in my surroundings. I went back to the office, minimized the card game, rubbed my eyes, and noticed the cards from Agent Bowe-Pitt and Banko Juarez.

And then something occurred to me. It was a ridiculous something, but it was better than nothing. As my *bubbe* used to tell me, *Az es zenen nito keyn andere mayles, iz a zumer-shprinkele oykh a mayle.*

If a girl has no other virtues, even a freckle can be considered one.

I had just such a freckle, one I was betting Detective Bean had not noticed.

Chapter 6

Banko Juarez was staying in the relatively new, inexpensive Page One Hotel on Commerce Street. The name had nothing to do with newspapers—I wasn't sure how many of the clients would've gotten the reference anyway. It was all about making sure guests were reachable via all media "24/7 and beyond," which, of course, made no sense. The gimmick was, if someone came to see you, even if you were out, the front desk texted you. That included vice cops, I guessed, given the girls I saw parked in the bar and the *alter kakers* bellying up to chat with them. There were also young people who had rented the multi-bed specials I saw advertised on a little billboard out front: a no-frills room with up to six cots.

I had called the etheric cleanser and made a $150-an-hour appointment to stop by the Page One at six. I also checked his website. Banko appeared to be a serious student of all things astral and beyond. He had posted videos and essays and financed his studies by going around the country by public transportation—vehicles that were also labs, I deduced—and doing his number on peoples' energy centers. It sounded like a lot of Sanskrit-cum-Buddhist mumbo jumbo to me, but then, I'm sure that a stranger observing an Orthodox Jewish service would feel exactly the same, seeing the men swaying, speaking aloud, and then whispering, all of them turned out in their finest Hebraic wardrobe with *tallit* over their shoulders and stringy *tzitzis* under their shirts and *tefillin* draped on their arms and heads.

There were no house phones at the Page One. The desk announced all visitors. Banko told the buxom concierge with pale skin and straight black hair that reached her shoulders and screamed "wig" to send me up to 816, on the top floor.

"Ah, the penthouse suite," I said to the young woman, whose name tag said Bananas.

"They are all penthouses with the lights out," she said, with a deep southern drawl that surprised me. I wondered if that was part of their advertising campaign.

"I'll take your word for it," I said.

"If you would ever like to—" she began seductively.

"Not my inclination," I said.

She smiled politely. "Nor mine, honey. I was going to say if you would ever like to visit our other spiritual guests, let me know. We have a group discount."

"Clever. Who would these others be?" I asked because I was really, really curious who the other parts of this package deal would be.

"There is an acupuncturist who specializes in opening the libido and a hypnotist whose field is sexual inhibition and past-life regressions."

"I didn't know the two were linked," I remarked.

"Everything is linked to sex," Bananas suggested.

"Even your name," I said.

She smiled overly sweetly. "That is my name. I was born to a poor mom who earned her living making banana fritters. Grew it into a nice business."

"I see. Well, that's quite a team upstairs," I admitted, getting out of that little faux pas. "Do you punch a card or something?"

"No," she smiled. "I remember faces."

I stopped by the convenient ATM machine in the corner before going up. My face was red and my neck flushed from having inadvertently insulted the concierge. I couldn't wait to get out of the lobby, but I had to wait for a well-dressed, chunky older man to finish pulling five hundred bucks in twenties from the machine. I wondered what he was getting for that. It seemed high just for an hour of sex, low for a night's worth. But as a sixty-minute time machine? Maybe it was a bargain.

This guy, in his fifties, gets to feel like he did when

he was in his twenties, only the girl has no hard-stops. It's not just a time machine but an alternate universe machine, where Mr. Three Piece Suit is an irresistible young stud.

That could be an ad campaign for a new credit card: MasterCardAndSubmissive or BangOfAmerica. *"We give you credit for studliness."* If only the law would get out of my way, I could turn the economy around in a week.

I went upstairs with enough cash for the hour, though if the etheric cleanser was as sincere as his website claimed, I had a feeling I could convince him to give me a bunch of extra hours for free.

Banko opened the door a moment before I knocked. That didn't surprise me: the elevator had a particularly loud "bing," no doubt to let occupants know that a guest had just arrived. Banko shut the door and followed me in. There were candles on the night tables, the wicks blackened. The air smelled of vanilla. I noticed the computer was active on the desk, with a jagged green line scrolling right to left like a polygraph.

"Is that me?" I asked.

"Yes indeed," he said. "I isolated it from the vibrations at the deli. It told me you were here."

"You didn't hear the elevator?"

"Of course. But that could have been anyone."

I bent in front of the laptop. This whole thing could be for show. The line could belong to anyone. "Has this been a profitable visit for you?"

"I don't make a lot, but I don't lose anything,"

he said. "Unless I stand around talking." He said that with a little laugh.

"Right." I rose, pulled the money from my front pocket, counted out an hour's worth, and put it on the desk. "I'm not here for a cleansing."

He stood by the little kitchen area, which had the minibar, sink, and coffeepot. "What do you want?"

"Did you hear what happened after you left?"

"No," he replied. Banko seemed genuinely perplexed.

I told him what had occurred and that maybe the police had not contacted him yet because he had paid in cash and they were looking at credit receipts first. He did not seem alarmed by the prospect of being interviewed, though I told him that, too, was not why I had come.

"I need to know, just between us, if this stuff is real."

Banko looked at me suspiciously. "Why would you think otherwise?"

"For one thing, the hotel has you bundled with an acupuncturist and a hypnotist," I said. "For another, I worked on Wall Street. I assume everyone's selling snake oil."

"Is that what I was doing in your restaurant? Putting on a show? Did you see me passing out business cards or soliciting business?" He was a little indignant. It didn't seem to be an act. He shook his head. "Civilians."

"Say again?"

"You lump everyone together. New agers, yogis,

ghost hunters, alien abductees. It's all the same crazy soup to you."

"Hey, the hotel did it. Now who's generalizing?"

He came over, swept up the money, handed it back. "I am not responsible for how the hotel 'bundles' its services. *My* research is real. The planes below and above the astral are real. Etheric cleansing is real. You can have that for free."

"I don't want it for free," I told him. "I want it to be real. I need it. I just wanted to be sure."

The hand with the money remained extended. His expression remained suspicious, guarded. "Explain."

"My explanation has two parts. First: it's possible that someone involved in the shooting was in my restaurant this morning, casing it out."

"Why is that possible?"

"Because the police believe it," I said. "But let's assume it's true. You might have recorded that individual on your computer. There could be an elevated spike, like you just said you saw with my arrival."

"I *did* see it."

"Yes, sorry. Anyway, that's part number one. Part number two is a little more interesting. Did you ever try matching someone's etheric lines?"

He hesitated before answering, the pale blue eyes hooding over. Maybe crashing in a hooker hotel had put him on guard against entrapment.

"This is on the level," I said. I took out the photo of the flyer. "The police found these stuck to trees along a stretch of highway. I thought, if you're on the level and we drive around that part of town, it's possible we might ID whoever put them up. You could make legal history, getting a conviction based on someone's etheric readout."

Banko took the photo from me. He read the flyer, shook his head slowly. "I don't like hate."

"Who *does*?"

"The haters," he replied. "They've got all this anger stored in their body, fueled by their chakras, their astral barriers trapping that like a psychological greenhouse effect. They get rid of it by hating."

He lost me at "chakras," but I was glad to see him engaged. I wasn't sure that my plan—if I could call it such, since it was as sketchy as a doodle—would get us anything other than driving around, calling attention to ourselves, and possibly drawing the SSS out as a result. Still, it was better than sitting at the deli playing solitaire.

"So I repeat my question," I said. "Have you ever tried it?"

He finally lowered his hand and looked at me. "Yes. In places like this."

"Sex motels?"

He nodded. "That's why I come here. This is much nicer than most, you know."

"I didn't, but that makes sense. It is in the heart of the city, not on some rural route."

"Upscale, downscale, it doesn't matter," he said. "Here, I get highly elevated readings—at night, downstairs, in the lobby, at the bar. Then I go down the halls and see if I can find those same individual etheric lines in the rooms."

"Wow. That's a little Peeping Tommy. Don't get me wrong, it's impressive, but also intrusive."

"Maybe, but I need the elevated energies to develop my next gen software."

"Why not go to a gym or a sports event?"

"I've tried going to arenas and stadia, but they don't let me use my laptop," he said. "At a gym I get physical exertion, but not elevated interpersonal connections. That's what I require to break through the astral barrier. The person-to-person connection."

I sighed. This was gibberish. It wasn't necessary that I understand it, but I wanted to. I pulled the chair from the desk. "Mr. Juarez, I've got you for another fifty minutes, give or take. I want you to explain this from the top in lay terms."

I sat. He paced as he spoke.

"You understand that we have energy, electrical impulses in our cells, in our muscles, in our minds."

I nodded. I remembered that much from high school biology. That and reproduction. As long as he didn't go anywhere near mitosis or the nitrogen cycle, we were good.

"Human beings have nine forms of existence," he went on. "There is, at the root of everything, the etheric plane. That's the ideal form of 'you' inside your mother's womb. It includes all your genetic information, residue from past lives—or racial memory, if you prefer—stored in your mother and all the positive energy your parents provide while you're in the womb. Your physical body is poured into that etheric shape. So you've got the physical plane and the etheric plane, and on top of those are the emotional and mental planes. Those are all packed inside a shell we call the astral plane. Got that?"

"I do." And I did. I could buy the etheric stuff—it sounded a lot like a soul to me—and the rest I knew I had. Maybe not in harmony, but I knew they were there.

"The astral plane is sort of where the 'self' ends and interactions with others begin," he said. "Beyond that are planes we don't need to get into now, aspects of ourselves that deal with all of humankind and the cosmos. My area of interest is what gets through the astral barrier. In order to communicate with others, even to simply look at them, we expend or take in energy. That has a particular color, a particular vibration. It can be measured."

"How?"

"As I told you this morning, by me."

"Oh, right. You've trained yourself to receive?"

"More like 'to trap.' When my hands are cupped, like so"—he held them as if he were holding a crown waist high, contemplating his ascension to the throne—"I sample the energy that's around me. There is a sensor in my USB port that reads me."

"How?"

"It's got several ant-like antennae suspended in the center," he said. "They vibrate when I do. I wrote the program and built the plug-in. It's pretty impressive."

"Sounds like it," I said, trying to hide my renewed dubiousness over fluttering hairs and a sudden feeling that this was a *behema*-sized waste of time. But there was always the way, way outside chance it could work.

"I gather your program matches incoming etheric energy with whatever you've recorded?"

"Exactly. What's great is that it doesn't even have to filter out my own vibrations because those are part of the original recordings."

"That *is* great," I said, hoping I didn't sound too sarcastic. "Do you have any appointments for tonight?"

"One, at seven. She 'liked' my Facebook page, saw that I would be here. I get at least one gig from that in every city I visit."

"God bless social media," I said. Actually, that got me thinking: I wondered if I could just 'like' the High Holy Days so I wouldn't have to go to temple, deal with the crowds. "Do the vibrations have to be fresh?"

"You mean, recent? As in, the person having been in a place lately?"

I nodded.

"No, they have to be there now. The device simply isn't sophisticated enough to record energy residue. I'm not one of those idiot ghost hunters."

"Right." It was marginally reassuring to know that even among these kooks there was a pecking order of craziness. "So what do you think about going out there, seeing if we can pick up the vibrations of bad guys who may be in the area?"

"For what kind of fee?"

"Free."

He made a face. I didn't.

"What you get from this experiment is proof that your system can be used in crime fighting," I told him. "If that happens, I see a reality TV series in your future."

He stopped pacing as he considered the proposition. "Hmm. That *is* a possibility, isn't it?"

"Damn right."

He thought a moment more. "All right. I'll do it."

"Swell. I've got a sympathy call to make. How about I pick you up at nine?"

"All right. Where are we going?"

"Hadley Park, off Interstate 40," I said. "A place where there are eleven trees."

"Sounds a little vague."

"It isn't really," I told him. "The foliage is grouped close together there, pretty easy to count."

"You're sure?"

"Positive."

"Fine. I'll meet you out front so you don't have to sit in the lobby," he said.

"Why? Maybe I could make a few bucks."

Banko wasn't sure whether or not I was kidding. I assured him I was. I think. When you marry or date men who think that all women should be geishas, handmaidens, or mute, when you hang around after those first warning signs and let your self-esteem erode, the aftershocks continue to be destructive, not constructive. Even after the ties are broken. You want to burn off your own skin, keep the pain close, reinforce how low this man made you feel so you don't do it again.

And then you stupidly date the same man or another one just like him, at least several more times.

I left the hotel to return to the martial arts school. Maybe I had been distracted or a little numb or just worn out by the day's events, but as I walked along the street something alarming occurred to me.

What if Banko was the person who had been casing out the deli?

I was taking him to a remote area assuming that he meant me no harm. But what if he was some kind of loon who went from town to town doing etheric *and* ethnic cleansing? Maybe I should—

What, call Grant to come with? Didn't you just decry women who do stupid things with men? You might as well just paint yourself as a plastic sex doll without a voice box and ride in the backseat for when he needs you.

What about Detective Bean or Agent Bowe-Pitt?

No. Southern bad guys, who have a tradition of running moonshine, lynching people, and making city boys squeal like pigs, have a sixth sense for John Law.

What about calling the whole thing off and doing what law enforcement suggested, just vegging out at the deli?

I snorted at that. Since leaving New York, my life had been about taking chances. Some of them were major but reasonable, like leaving the city in the first place; some were insane, like this. But they all lit fires in me, and there was no denying they were all part of the Gwen Katz drumbeat now, for better or worse, richer or poorer, alive or dead.

I had just turned the corner onto 5th Avenue N and was admitting to myself that I was a little bit excited about the nuttiness of trying to find a killer with bug-hair sensors, when I was distracted by movement to my right and what seemed like a bird flying into my face. It was followed by a strange smell, amber-colored swirls, and my knees turning to mush before I went unconscious.

Chapter 7

I came to in a vehicle. I knew it was a vehicle because I was moving, not because I could see. My baseball cap was pulled way low over my eyes so that the brim rested on my nose. My hands were cuffed behind me. They hurt, a lot, because whoever had abducted me had thoughtfully secured me with the seat belt. That left the small of my back pressed against the metal cuffs. I could feel my cell phone in my back pocket. I shifted a little. The one time I *wanted* to butt-dial, I couldn't.

Which I realized, as I came around, was probably the least of my worries. I was dizzy with a wicked headache. I didn't feel nauseous, and that was too bad. I really wanted to puke on whoever had jumped out at me with a handkerchief—which was probably the "bird" I saw—and drugged me.

I recalled the dead girlfriend of the African-American cop. Yet, oddly, I wasn't afraid. There was no one to ransom me to, and if someone wanted to kill me I probably wouldn't be alive now.

"I'm really not comfortable," I announced.

Someone, a woman, said something that sounded Asian. Someone answered. I was against the driver's side door. The woman was sitting to my right. The second man was in front, driving. The woman spoke again, this time in English.

"I am sorry that this was necessary," she told me.

"Fine. Can you just remove the seat belt? I won't try to get out the door. My hands are cuffed."

"We will let you leave when you tell us what Chan said to you."

"He said he wanted one of our standard platters."

"Were there any special requests?"

"Such as?"

"*Any?*"

"No."

"No special food?"

"None."

"Did he indicate he was going to buy anything else to serve?"

"Like what? Dessert?"

"*Anything,*" the interrogator said, more harshly.

"Nothing."

"Did he carry anything from any other restaurant or market?"

"No!" I said, wondering how many ways they

could come at this. "He was carrying nothing whatsoever."

"Tell us everything he said. He called you first."

I didn't know if that was a question or a statement. If it were a statement, then someone knew he called; these people could have been from his school. Perhaps they overheard him. Or someone at the school called someone else. If it were a question, then it could still be someone at the school—just someone who wasn't there at eight-thirty in the morning.

"Sifu Chan called and told me he was having belt promotions," I said. "I thought he was talking about belts that hold your pants up, and he corrected me. I asked if I could talk to him after the breakfast rush. He said he would stop by at ten-thirty. That was the entirety of our conversation on the phone."

"You called him *sifu*. Had you known him before?"

"No."

"Are you certain?"

"It's the *truth*," I said, exasperated.

"All right. After the call?"

"He stopped by at ten-thirty. I had the cook prepare some food samples. He made his selection in about a minute. Then we talked about how he had a school in Manhattan, in Chinatown, and that he left because he didn't want to train gang members—"

"Did he mention any names?"

"No."

"Any affiliations in New York?"

"No!"

"All right. Go on."

"He said he had been here six months, that he came to Nashville because he liked the music. We discussed his favorite Johnny Horton song, "The Battle of New Orleans," and then he was dead."

The two resumed speaking in whatever language they were speaking. I felt like I was a kid again, listening to my grand-relatives speaking Yiddish. Of course, I wasn't cuffed and blindfolded back then, just ignored. Oddly, it felt surprisingly similar, the Old World attitude that under no circumstances did children need to know the business of their elders. As if I would have understood, at seven or eight, whatever the hell they were talking about. But I guess their parents did it to them, on and on back through history. When your own children are considered outsiders, imagine what outsiders are considered. Maybe I was facing a little of that circling of the wagons here. These might be nothing more than Asian restaurateurs *hockin me a chinick* because I was an outsider who was suddenly a threat to their core clientele.

I didn't really think that, but in a world where a matzo ball is shot from the end of a fork anything is possible.

"Why did you go to the school this afternoon?" the woman asked.

I got my brain back in the game. I said I went to pay a sympathy call, told her who I spoke with, who I laid eyes on, what I said, and everything else that had happened in the space of that four or five minutes. I even mentioned the police officer. I wondered if that surprised them. Or if they had been watching the school. Or if he had been reporting to them. I had plenty of facts but shockingly little information.

"He placed an order with you," the voice said. "How was it paid for?"

"Credit card."

"Signed how?"

"With a pen—"

"*In what language? With what name?*

"Jesus, I honestly don't know!"

"Who has the receipts?"

"The police," I said. "They took them all."

I felt something like a beesting under my chin. The stinger didn't go away. It was the point of a very, very sharp knife. My Ginsu crack had come back to haunt me.

"What are you not telling us?" the woman asked.

"Nothing," I said. "I have no dog in this fight. I don't know anything about Mr. Chan's past or his connections or his school or his family. Nothing!"

I managed to get that out just before my heart kicked up the pace and my arms began to wobble like water-filled balloons. Was this their parting Hail Mary maneuver, or was this phase two of what would prove a long, painful, disfiguring interrogation?

The knife punctured flesh and twisted slightly. That hurt.

"There is always more," the woman told me. "Think."

"Take that out of my throat and I'll try."

She pushed it a little harder. So much for that tactic. My mind quickly grew sharper than the blade.

"The napkin holder," I said.

"What?"

"In the deli, before the gunshot, I think he stared at the napkin holder. For about a second or two."

"Why?"

"I don't know."

"*Why?*"

Another twist of that blade, the pain way out of proportion with its size. Nasty electric waves shot up and down my jaw all the way to my ears. I whimpered. I had been attacked by a guy with a knife, once, and cut. But that was sudden. This pain, coming on top of the previous pain, was sharper. My vulnerability was greater, the reality of death so close I felt I could say *shalom* to my mother and Uncle Murray.

The woman wanted me to speculate. Okay. I could do that.

"Look, at first I thought he was staring at the matzo ball. He had just inverted this little shrimp fork with some kind of finger maneuver, he stabbed the matzo ball he had been looking at, and then he picked it up and kept looking at it. When his eyes didn't move I thought that maybe he *wasn't* looking at the matzo ball but at the polished side of the dispenser, seeing something behind him. I could be wrong about both of those things. He might have been daydreaming. Maybe he had gas from the food he had eaten before that. It can happen if you're not used to it. Or he could have been looking at the plate, savoring the aroma of the food, thinking of something he should ask me. He could have been wondering if he locked the door at home. I don't know. I swear, *I don't know.*"

"You said he had been coming from home."

"Yes—I mean, I think so. He called from a cell phone, not a landline. The name on my caller ID was May Wong."

"Auntie May?"

"I don't know. The only Aunt May I know is in the Spider-Man movies. He said he would stop by on his way to the school. I assumed he was at home. That's it. That's *all* I remember."

The knife relaxed slightly. I didn't. My calf muscles were so tight I thought my skin would burst. I was pushing up from the floor, relaxing the pressure on my hands, raising my throat from the blade.

The knife remained where it was, except when the car went over bumps in what was apparently now a dirt road. I got repeated pricks, each one accompanied by a painful spark in my chin.

"One more time," the woman said. "How did he sign the receipt? Was it in English or Chinese?"

I was starting to get angry or panic. Probably both. I replayed that moment with Ken Chan on the back of my eyelids. No difference. No revelation.

"I. Don't. Know," I told her.

More non-English was spoken. The knife point was removed from my throat. The seat belt was undone. Something was pressed into my left hand. The car stopped. The door opened. I was helped out. I stood there half-waiting for someone to come up behind me and cut my throat. That wasn't an idle fear: I was so afraid, based on the zero concern the woman had demonstrated for my comfort or pain, that I had difficulty standing. It was only after I realized they had left me with the key to the handcuffs that I calmed down a little—only then I had other problems. How was I going to put it in the slot? I was terrified of dropping it in what felt like ankle-high grass. With the blindfold still on, I'd really be screwed.

I listened for traffic. There wasn't any. Then I remembered the cell phone in my pocket. I managed to hook it out with the index finger of my right hand. I got it from my pocket. And dropped it. I swore.

I felt around for it with my foot. I found it. I lightly stepped on it, then dropped to my knees on hard ground. It hurt, though I was quickly distracted by the wrenching pain in my wrists and the trickle of blood running down my throat into my bra.

A tinny, tiny voice came from the phone. "Hello?"

"This is Gwen Katz," I shouted.

"I know—I saw your name on my—"

"Who is this?"

"Huh?"

"I was abducted. I'm tied up. Who did I just call?"

"It's me, Banko. What do you mean you were abducted?"

"Someone kidnapped me outside your hotel," I shouted. "I need help."

"Where are you?"

"I don't know. Listen, I'm going to try and get the blindfold off. Don't go anywhere, okay?"

"Sure. Of course."

The easiest thing would have been to lean forward and rub my forehead on the ground to try and tug the thing off. But if I fell, if I couldn't push up off my forehead, I wouldn't be able to get up. Instead, I walked around, taking tentative steps forward, hoping to bump into a post or a tree. I found the latter and put my face up against it. The cloth snagged on a broken-off branch, and I was able to work it down around my nose. A few head shakes and it fell to my throat. I looked around.

I was in the yard of a foreclosed house in the middle of nowhere. I walked over to the mailbox. The address was faded but legible. Knight

Drive Extension, Number 917. I strode back to the phone and told Banko.

"Would you do me a favor and call that in directly to Detective Jill Bean?"

"Absolutely," he said. "I'm hanging up now so I can call."

"Okay," I said. "Thanks a lot."

He clicked off, and I stepped on the phone to disconnect. Who knew that cell phones were step-sensitive. Could be a selling point.

It was dusk, but it was still bright enough for me to see cats moving in the grasses. The good thing about that was they'd keep the field mice away. I fidgeted with the key and tried to put it into the lock, but that wasn't happening. I used my chin to try to stuff the blindfold into my wounded throat, but that was also going nowhere. Still groggy from the chloroform, I leaned against the tree, listening to the wind, not sure I wanted someone to come along before the police arrived. There was my very strong desire for freedom versus the loss of dignity inherent in my helplessness. There was the idea of someone fussing over me, which I hate, along with the possibility that it could be some redneck who'd decide that this was the perfect time and place to court a bound Jewish chick. In short, there were no scenarios that really made me happy right now.

I distracted myself by pre-answering the questions I thought Detective Bean might ask. *Do you have any idea who did this?* No.

Would you recognize any of the voices if you heard them again? Possibly.

Can you describe anything about the car? I thought about that one. No air freshener. No music. Engine sounded well-tuned. So apart from the shoulder-strap seat belt and the auto-lock that I heard open all the doors at once, no.

Did you hear or smell anything that might give us a clue—any food, perfume? No. I had the smell of chloroform in my nose, along with the odor of whatever fabric softener was used on the handkerchief—which, I noticed as I looked down, was soaking up more blood than I wanted to see outside my body. I wondered if I should be lying down instead of standing. Upright, wasn't my heart working harder to push blood to my brain?

I didn't know. I had this sudden, weird vision of dying as a properly prepared kosher victim. That gave me a strangely comforting feeling as I felt the damp, sticky cloth growing damper and stickier against my collarbone. And there was probably some justice to it, I told myself, after all the glatt meals I'd served since coming here.

My light-headed reverie ended as I heard sirens and saw a pair of flashing lights descending on the site. Detective Bean wasn't coming alone. One of the red strobes punctuating the twilight seemed a little higher than the other. I hoped an ambulance was part of the little convoy.

It was. The police car, which was in front, went

off-road and directed the ambulance to do the same.

Right, I thought. *Tire tracks in the dirt.*

I walked groggily toward my phone so I wouldn't forget it. I dropped back to my knees where I saw the battery light glowing, intending to pick it up with my teeth. In retrospect, that was a stupid idea—but then, I wasn't thinking too clearly about anything. Instead, as I bent toward it, the dark grasses spun, the lights of the ambulance twirled a bit, and I landed on my face, unconscious.

Chapter 8

It was odd to wake up for the third time in a single day.

The ambulance was just pulling up to the emergency entrance at Vanderbilt University Medical Center when I came to. I was light-headed but aware as I was sped through a room to a curtained area and moved to a bed. I answered a bunch of questions a nurse asked about what I could see—"The light you're shining in my eyes"—whether I had feeling in my hands and toes, whether I felt nauseous.

An IV was poked into the back of my right hand, and then a doctor came over and looked under some bandages on my throat.

"I'm Dr. Nusses," he said. "You are—?"

"Gwen Katz."

"Hi, Gwen. You're going to need a few stitches to close that cut. If you'll tilt your head back," he said, as he tilted my head back, "we can have you patched up in no time."

"Suture self," I said, having no idea what part of my brain that came from.

It was pretty quick and surprisingly painless, thanks to whatever they used to dope me up and swab the skin. I wondered if I'd have one of those sexy scars or an ugly one. Turned out that with two stitches I wouldn't have any scar to speak of. In fact, a nurse told me I'd pretty much stopped bleeding in the ambulance. They just had to be sure.

When they were finished, Grant came to see me. I wasn't surprised. Someone had to interview me, and I suspected he would pull rank. Seeing his head come around the slip in the curtain made me tense up. Remember what I said about people fawning over me? I liked it less when it came from a guy who was not especially simpatico unless someone *was* injured. And even then it had the reek of a police officer's trained bedside manner. I've said it before and here it is again: yes, I was being a hard-ass. Grant wasn't a bad man. Like me, he was all about his work. Unlike me, the way I was with customers is the way I am with everyone. The way Grant was with me is the way he was with women who had been robbed or were the victims of domestic violence. Behind his kindly face with soft eyes, the ones I fell for months ago, he was still a crime-solving machine. Unfortunately, after Phil and the other jerks scattered through my past, I didn't want to spend my time with "no cigar."

"Hey," he said.

"Hi," I rasped flatly.

"How are you?" he asked.

"Not as bad as I probably look," I said. I craned to the left, toward the little nightstand. "Is my phone there?"

He came in, handed it to me. "You look fine."

"Right."

"You up to answering a few questions?" he asked, with the smile I'd seen before and used to think was cute.

"Sure."

He pulled over a straight-backed chair and took a notepad from the pocket of his blazer— the clothbound little book he used to whip out and make notes in when we were supposed to be watching a DVD—and began asking the questions I had already asked myself. I answered them the same way. He added two that were obvious yet that I hadn't bothered to think of. The first one was if my abductors had gone through my pockets. I thought back. They had not. They were cautious.

The second question was more troubling.

"What were you doing in that neighborhood?" Grant asked.

It was a legitimate question, even though, coming from him, it felt like prying. I answered honestly. Sort of.

"I was visiting a friend."

"Where?"

"At the hotel. Isn't there street video?"

"Yes, of you turning the corner and leaving

the frame. Someone had cased out the street, knew where it was blind. Our guess is they were waiting between parked cars."

"We seem to have a lot of blind spots in the city's security."

"This isn't New York," he said defensively. "We don't have the money or need for a Ring of Steel." Grant looked at me with disapproval. "So?"

"So?" I repeated. "Think this is related to that gal who was abducted two weeks ago?"

"I don't know," he said. "First things first. I know your friends. None of them works at that hotel. I repeat: what were you doing there?"

"Did I say 'works'? Sometimes a hotel is just a hotel. He's from out of town, a little naive. He's rooming there."

Grant's expression told me he wasn't convinced. I didn't blame him. He knew me as well as I knew him. He let the matter rest—for now. "Were you coming or going?"

"Going."

"Where were you coming from?"

"I had visited Chan's kung fu school, I went home for an early dinner and then walked to the hotel."

"Were you aware of anyone watching you?"

"Only the cop who saw me leave the school."

"I mean after that. At the hotel. Outside or in the lobby."

I was about to ask him if he'd checked the security cameras when I realized there probably weren't any there either. The residents and clientele there would rather be mugged than photographed.

"I didn't notice anyone," I told him. "Given the other ladies with their blown hair and sprayed-on minis, anyone looking at me would've stood out."

Grant was like a mountain lion circling a wounded coyote. He wanted to pounce. Finally, he did. "I'd like the name of this individual you visited."

"No."

"Gwen, I will go there and talk to the clerk and find out one way or the other," he said. "It is an essential aspect of this investigation."

I wasn't keen on sharing that information with the police. Nashville is a city, but in many ways it's still a small town. I didn't want to get the reputation for being crazy in addition to everything else. But I couldn't dispute the possibility that he was right. After all, I really didn't know anything about Banko except what he'd told me. On the other hand, I didn't want Grant looking into Banko's etheric readings. I was dubious, but he'd be merciless.

"What time is it?" I asked.

He looked at his watch. "Ten past eight."

"I'll tell you what," I said. "I'm supposed to meet him in fifty minutes. Why don't you come with."

"Why can't you just tell me—"

"Because when I say come with, I mean come with us."

"Where?"

"To the highway where the flyers were put up."

"Why?"

"The guy I'm going with is sort of a spiritualist," I said, measuring my words. I didn't want Grant confiscating his computer under some evidentiary pretext. "He has a computer program he thinks can 'detect' bad people."

"Gwen, are you serious? Are you *sure* you're okay?" Those weren't questions, they were full-throated condemnations.

"I'm fine, Grant. Even if he's *meshugeneh,* I didn't want to sit around. Or lie around. I still don't. It seemed like an interesting idea."

"Like psychic detectives and cats who predict death by the way they wash their ears. I've heard it all, Gwen. And even if this wasn't BS, you shouldn't be nosing around where hate material was just posted. Go home, Gwen."

"I can't."

"Why? I'll take you there—you shouldn't be driving anyway."

"No, I mean I can't. Agent Bowe-Pitt of the FBI told me I should sleep in the deli with a police guard, not at the house."

Grant shook his head. "He's worried about white supremacist terrorists. I'm worried about keeping the body count at one. And you're—divining for electrical residue."

"It's more like elevated impulses, not residue."

"Whatever, it's ridiculous!"

I didn't respond. This had gone past police

work. It was our old dynamic of Grant being sure he was right. Even if he was, in this case, I liked being able to make choices without feeling like I had an adversary.

Grant told me to call if I thought of anything else or needed help if something went wrong on my "little adventure." Even that was dismissive. I will never understand how people, couples, however intelligent and rational, slide so quickly and utterly off the road of good intentions into old, familiar ruts.

Well . . . that was one way to get Grant off the scent.

Dr. Nusses returned to check my wound and vitals and told me I could leave, admonishing me to drink a lot of juice because of the blood I'd lost. I assured him I would. He gave me a prescription for painkillers in case the wound or the stitches hurt. The nurse returned, wheelchaired me to the desk so I could fill out all the paperwork. Then while the receptionist took a phone call, an orderly came and wheeled me to the street. He helped me up, made sure I was steady. He was very tall, looked like that basketball player Jeremy Lin—whom I followed while he briefly played for the New York Knicks, didn't care after that—and he had a nice smile.

"Would you like me to get you a cab?" he asked.

"They were kind enough to ask at the desk. I'm fine."

He locked the wheels and came around to the front of the chair. "May I have your phone?"

I handed it to him. He put in a number. "If you need anything, call."

"That's really kind, but I'm sure I'll be okay."

He handed it back. "Also, if it matters—and you can tell me it's none of my business—I believe in auras and spirits. Not like my grandma. She's real big into divination and tea leaves and all that. She swears by it. But I like to leave the door open to all kinds of things."

"You know what they say, 'There are more things in heaven and earth . . . ,'" I said blandly. But that was not the big, red-faced thought in my brain. "So—did everyone hear us talking back there?"

"We couldn't help it," he said. "Okay, that's a lie: we were listening. We love that stuff, and you two sound like you have a history."

"More like a collection of skirmishes without much of a narrative," I said.

He chuckled. "Well, we all thought he was being just a little intolerant. Even the guys thought that."

"Thanks," I smiled. "That's good to know."

"Well, take care of yourself," he said. "And don't push yourself."

"I'll try not to."

He spun the wheelchair around and walked back toward the hospital. "The sympathy call can wait until tomorrow."

The words hung in the air for a moment. Then I felt like I'd been hit on the back of the head with a boxing glove. "What did you say?" I asked, as I turned.

But he had already gone through the automatic glass doors. I looked into the lighted waiting area, with plastic chairs full of bleeding and aching patients getting the full measure of their spanking-new health care coverage. I thought back. I hadn't mentioned the sympathy call, I was sure of it. Grant hadn't either. I had mentioned Chan's school, that was all.

I went back into the ward, a little faster than I should have, and leaned on the counter as I asked the receptionist if I could speak with the orderly. She asked me which one. I told her. She said there was no tall Asian orderly.

I knew I hadn't hallucinated him. "Were people listening when I talked to the detective who came in?"

"Ms. Katz, no one has time to listen to anything here."

Damn, dammit, and damnation. Someone was watching back at the house where they left me . . . they were prepared. They saw the ambulance, saw the name on it, and got here first.

But why?

To hear what I'd tell the cops? It was the same thing I'd told them.

Then why confront me afterward? I hadn't told Grant anything useful. *Now* I had a face to attach to the abductors. All I had to do was—

I jumped as my phone beeped. I didn't recognize the number. It was local. I answered.

"Yes?"

"Ms. Katz, we did not realize you have a relationship with a police detective," the caller said. "Now we do."

It was the woman from the car. "So?" I asked. "Now you also know I didn't tell him anything more than I told you because I don't *know* anything."

"That is apparent," the caller said. "We suggest you let it go at that. You do not want to call Detective Daniels and tell him about the orderly. You do not want to give him this number, which, in any case, is from a disposable phone. Just go on your expedition tonight and forget about us."

"I'd like to," I said. "How do I know you'll forget about me?"

"Because this is our matter, not yours. You merely stumbled into it. Stumble out again." There was an "or else" in her voice that she promptly articulated: "Next time, we will not stop at a prick to the throat."

The caller hung up. I put the phone in my back pocket. I truly didn't know what ticked me off more at that moment: the fact that I had been—still might be—under surveillance by Asian thugs, or that the kid I thought was so sweet and caring had actually been pumping me for information and—*and*—had lifted my number while pretending to give me his.

The big chazer, I thought bitterly.

I guess they hadn't done that in the car because I was sitting on it. Or maybe they didn't want to leave fingerprints. I looked at the time on the phone. It was eight-thirty. I had just enough time to get my car and collect Banko Juarez. I wondered if I should bother, seeing as how it seemed that the Asians were my enemies and not the SSS.

When it comes to Jews being hated, one can never have too little paranoia, I decided. I already had a date with Banko, and it was worth checking out. Besides, as I started in the direction of the parking garage—propelled by equal parts of determination and anger—I found myself actually looking forward to the excursion.

Compared to everyone else around me right now, Banko seemed the most reliably grounded soul in my circle.

Chapter 9

I didn't have the clearest head in the world as I got behind the wheel, though I had stopped at the deli to load up on OJ. I also packed some bananas in case I needed a potassium fix. One of the things that surprised me, when I took over Murray's, was how many people had bodies that talked to them about very specific food needs. One customer claimed that her bones told her when they required milk. Another said the same thing about protein. Another said her teeth informed her when they needed egg matzo. All but that last one made at least a little sense.

With me it was potassium. Which meant that I ate more bananas than the average chimpanzee. I've read it's important in brain function, and I use mine a lot. That doesn't explain the chimps, but I'm sure there are environmental reasons. The point being, I always kept bags in the car for banana peels, and the car smelled of banana.

I never noticed it unless I was giving someone a ride.

"It smells like a monkey house in here," Banko said after he'd eased into the front seat, his computer open on his lap. He had brought something folded inside a pillowcase.

"I hope you mean the bananas," I replied.

"What else?"

"A girl worries about how she smells," I said.

"God, no. That isn't what I meant." But I noticed him sniff again, as though he were making sure. "No, you smell fine. The bananas smell fine too, I just don't expect them when I get in a car." He stared for a moment. "What happened to your throat?"

"Souvenir," I said. "My abduction. I can't talk about it. I'm fine." I didn't want to alarm him. "What's in the pillowcase?" I asked as I pulled away.

"The shower curtain," he said. "It felt like rain, so I checked the forecast."

"Have you always had a strong sense of smell and—what, touch?"

"They're something I've developed, along with my other senses. It helps in my work to be sensitive, obviously."

"What did you smell in the hotel lobby?" I was curious about what he would say, how honest he would be. Either the guy was a human bloodhound or he was full of it.

"I smelled wine," he said. "It's very strong there."

"Is that all?"

"Yes," he said. Then he added, "The hallways—
they're different. Especially outside the rooms."

Point to Banko. I let the subject drop.

"How was your session?" I asked.

"Interesting," Banko replied. "I can't tell you
about it, of course. My work is confidential. It's
like being a doctor."

"I understand," I said.

"I will tell you this, though. It was my first
transgender subject, a male-bodied female.
It's going to be interesting analyzing those
readings."

"A male-bodied female being a pre-op trans-
sexual? Someone who's going to become a female-
bodied former male-bodied female?"

"That's right."

Like Lou Costello in "Who's On First," I
wasn't even sure what I had just said. This was
like the rabbit hole down which everything
kept getting stranger. As with my previous
remarks about neologisms, the plethora of
sexual identities, foreign-American affiliations,
and hyphenates in general had grown exponen-
tially in recent memory and kept getting larger.
Technically, I was a former-New-York-woman-
Jew-thirtysomething-divorcée-restaurateur-
bananaphile. How many defining qualities would
be elevated to nom-de-guerre prominence before
the language buckled from the weight?

Or my menu, I thought. I couldn't imagine
having to list, as part of the name of each dish,
every ingredient to which someone might be

allergic or intolerant, along with the calorie count and, oh yeah, the name. That was when all of life would become like those fast-spoken qualifiers in TV ads for pharmaceuticals.

It was a moonless, overcast night, which meant that the glow of the computer screen would make us anything but stealthy. Banko suggested we go right to the spot where the flyers had been posted to see what he and the computer picked up.

I got off the interstate and drove toward the park. I had taken a little time to read up on the history of the place, and I understood why the hate group had picked it to post its signs. The thirty-four acres used to belong to the John L. Hadley plantation. In 1912 Nashville bought the property, and it became the first public park created especially for African-Americans. What seems, through a modern lens, to be overtly segregationist was considered quite forward-thinking at the time.

We parked on Alameda Street, where there were several other cars. I grabbed a windbreaker I had in the backseat and slipped it on, and put my cell phone in my pocket. We walked along the western rim of the park, toward Tennessee State University. It had begun to drizzle, and hunched against the rain, Banko held the stuffed pillowcase over the computer.

"Where are we headed?" he asked.

"To the corner of John A. Merritt Boulevard,"

I told him. "That's where Mapquest showed the trees to be."

I hadn't wanted to park right on top of them in case anyone was there . . . or watching. The rain actually felt good, like cool, misty kisses on my still-groggy forehead. Also, my throat felt better with my face turned upward, the skin extended. The bandage had pinched a little as I drove. Not now.

I saw the trees through the drizzle. "There they are."

Banko squinted ahead. "I can set up anywhere— let's go to the bench by the tennis courts."

The courts were between us and the trees. We stayed on the sidewalk. The courts passed to my right like freighters moving by a skiff—big, monolithic, impersonal. It struck me that many places required people to acquire a personality. Even monuments. When I worked on Wall Street, I often had lunch in Battery Park and sat facing the Statue of Liberty. In my brain, I always saw it with returning troop carriers after World War Two, with boatloads of immigrants passing en route to nearby Ellis Island, of fireworks on the Fourth of July. It was never just the big, green statue. If it were, I would remember which foot was forward, whether her feet were bare, how long her sleeves were.

The tennis courts were behind us as we turned the corner. There was a dreamy haze under the streetlamp. We went to a new metal bench that faced the trees. Banko used the pillowcase to wipe the dampness from the seat, then spread the clear shower curtain over us like it was a snowy-day Jets game. The computer glowed brightly, ethereally under the shroud. While my companion tapped buttons, I looked out at the university. Was it possible that students had put the flyers up? And if so, was it some kind of provocative hazing ritual or in earnest? Campuses weren't just about political correctness. They were about free speech and self-expression. For all I knew. they had some kind of totally legitimate historical or socio-political club called When We Were White or The Ideals of the Confederacy. The perps could even be professors. God knows the one I had some recent dealings with, Reynold Sterne, was a diabolical, self-absorbed eccentric. And he might be one of the milder cases. Academia was a haven for crazies.

The graph was back on the computer. It was strange to think how different things had been the last time I saw that screen. We were about twenty feet from the trees, and Banko cupped his hands around the sides of the computer as he had done before. He was obviously concentrating, so I didn't ask what I was looking at. There were two lines, which were us. They were pretty straight, apparently reflecting our repose. Apparently, there were no lingering energies here. Not even from the tennis courts. I gave myself a mental kick in the *tuchas* for imagining that there could be anything to this.

"Look," Banko said quietly.

A third line had come on as a short spike. I looked ahead, didn't see anyone. I snaked from under the shelter and looked back. I didn't see anyone there either. I glanced back at the computer. A fourth and fifth line had appeared.

"Too bad there isn't a compass on this thing," I muttered.

Banko shifted his hands so they were both angled to the left at about forty-five degrees. The spikes softened. He moved his hands back to where they had been, fingertips toward the university. The spikes sharpened again.

"Oh," I said.

The energy was coming from the university. Now I saw three people gather under an eave across the street, all of them smoking cigarettes. This was insane. The gadget actually worked.

I turned my eyes back to the trio as I saw the cigarettes get tossed aside. The figures were still there, a silhouette against the lighter darkness of the building behind them. After a moment, one of them came toward us. Banko was busy watching the lines and focusing his hands or whatever he did. I was starting to think it was a good time to get back to the car. I was about to tug on Banko's arm when the computer pinged.

"There's a match," he said. "One of these lines was at your deli that morning."

It wasn't unusual for students to come to Murray's. We had discount cards for students.

There was a sixth line now and a smaller

seventh: someone was out walking their little wiener dog to our left.

"This is amazing," I said. The dog walker's lines strengthened, while two of the other three held steady. The third was jaggedly bolder. I looked through the filmy drizzle. The figures from the campus had stopped under a tree on the other side of Merritt. The dog walker's gaze lingered on us, probably trying to figure out what the hell we were doing out on a wet night with electronics. He continued to the east under his umbrella.

It was rain now, no longer drizzle, and water was starting to run around the overhead lip of the shower curtain.

"We should probably go," Banko said.

I was about to insist on the same thing, albeit for a different reason. Banko was so into his ethericism he forgot we came here to find bad guys. These men were not just lines on a graph; they were people, and they were near. We stood, Banko wrapping his computer in the plastic shroud, just as the men from the campus decided to cross the street. They weren't walking, they were running. I had to know why.

I decided suddenly, impulsively—as I do most things—to stand my ground. I had come here to find out about a killer. The dog walker was still within earshot; there was still occasional vehicular traffic. If this man and his friends were bent on mischief, they wouldn't do anything here—I hoped.

One would think, with all the knives I own, that I would have thought to bring one. Or a handgun. My uncle had owned a .38. It was in the safe in my office. I had not bothered to obtain a license, had never fired it, had never even held it except to check that it wasn't loaded. So that wasn't in my pocket either. All I had in the windbreaker were my hand and my cell phone. I took it out. I had a 911 app that took a picture and sent it to the police. That was useful in my business. I had my thumb at the ready as I pointed the phone ahead.

The three men arrived with a splat of feet on the sidewalk followed by a *squoosh* as they ran into the park. I turned on a flashlight app so I could see them. They were wearing security uniforms. They all squinted and shielded their eyes like vampires confronting a cross. One of the men turned a flashlight on me. It was a standoff in two wet, white beams. I shut mine. The man did not.

"We've had some trouble here," he said in a cigarette-sandpapered drawl. "We wanted to make sure everything was okay."

"It was. It is," I said. "Would you switch off the searchlight?"

He obliged. I saw a big bluish blob where his head should be. They were keeping their distance, still just dark shapes in the night.

"You're not a student," the man went on.

"I'm not on college property. What's this about?"

They talked quietly among themselves, like the witches in *Macbeth*. I would have left, only I was interested to see where this went. From his anxious backing-away and shifting from foot to foot, Banko was way less intrigued.

"There's been trouble out here," one of the men said. "We were just making sure you weren't in danger."

"Thanks, we're fine. What kind of trouble?"

"Vandalism."

"Have you seen any of the vandals?" I asked. "Any idea who they are?"

The men hesitated. "Is that why you're here?" one of them asked.

"Is *what* why I'm here?"

"Investigating? You two reporters or something? Bloggers?"

"No."

The rain kicked up a notch, and we were all getting soaked. The three men were a featureless blur. They had not done or said anything overtly intimidating. but that hulking silhouette was hostile nonetheless.

"I know you," one of the men said suddenly. "You took over the Jewish deli from Murray Katz."

"That's right. He was my uncle."

"Well, you should probably leave," the man said.

"Why?" I asked defiantly.

"Because smart people don't stand in the rain," he said.

"Any other reason?" I asked.

"Smart people watch out when there's a storm," he added. That was more pointed, more menacing.

The man didn't say anything else. He lingered a moment, and then they turned to go in segments, like a caterpillar. I watched them run back to the campus. I didn't realize that my hands were tight balls at my side until I finally released them.

Banko brushed hair from his eyes and came back to my side. He was hugging his well-protected computer to his chest and bending over it. "Jesus. What was that about?"

"I'm not sure," I admitted. "They were itchy about something. Let's get the hell out of here."

Banko nodded enthusiastically. I turned and jumped back, nearly knocking my companion over. Someone was approaching from around the tennis courts. A man with a trench coat and an umbrella. I stood where I was, water pulling my hair along my neck and soaking my bandage.

"Care to get under?" the man said, as he came forward. It was Grant.

I stayed where I was. "Dammit, did you follow me?"

"The NPD has a murder to solve," he said. "We're not convinced you weren't the target."

"So the answer is yes."

"You're getting drenched—"

"It's just water," I said. "I can just wipe that off."

"Nice," he said.

"You could at least have told me what you were doing."

"You can't have it both ways, Gwen," he said. "Either we're friends, or I'm just a cop doing his job."

I couldn't argue with that. And there's no disputing that I'm not at my best when I'm soaked and on edge. I resisted telling him that I was going to take Banko back to the hotel, then crash at the deli. That would just sound cranky, and besides, he'd have to follow me anyway if he were concerned about me being shot. With a short, deep sigh I started back to the car—

There was a muddy thud at my side, followed by a soft crack. Grant pushed me back and I hit the muck with a sickening sense of déjà vu. Behind me, I heard something crunch, like gears; it was followed by a clattering. I had no idea what it was and didn't take the time to check.

"Down!" he shouted at Banko. Grant was sprawled on top of me and couldn't get to my companion.

Grant wore his radio in his belt. Even as I tried to understand what exactly was happening, he was calling for assistance. Time oozed by. I felt him crawl over me to make sure my head was covered. I turned my face sideways so I could breathe. He did not place his weight on me, not entirely; I could feel him raised up at the chest, probably looking in the direction from which the shot had come.

"You okay?" I asked Banko, who was lying beside me.

"Yeah, though I'm not sure about the laptop."

We stopped talking. I could hear Grant breathing, feel Banko breathing, realized I wasn't. I took a breath. We waited like rabbits in a field, frozen, waiting for the farmer who'd had it to blow us away. Since I'm not a farmer and never have been, I wondered why I thought of that analogy. I remembered a story a great-great someone once told me of their farm in a Ukrainian shtetl, how they had to fight the local hare population for crops.

It could have been thirty seconds or five minutes that passed. I didn't know. All I knew was that there wasn't a second shot. Only when we heard sirens did Grant get up, and only then did I realize how cold and thoroughly soaked with rain and mud I was. Suction was actually holding me to the ground, and I needed a hand from Grant to get up.

"Don't go near the impact site," he said, pointing to the right. "We'll want to get pictures, figure trajectory."

As I flopped onto my relatively dry tush, he handed me the umbrella, and now I took it. Banko literally crawled over, dragging the muck-saturated shower curtain beside him. He sat beside me with a sigh as he pulled the laptop from the plastic. The monitor part had snapped from the base on the left side, and water and mud had seeped in.

"How's your device?" I asked.

"It's safe. I removed it before I packed the computer away."

"What about the data?"

"Everything we got tonight is probably gone," he said. "The rest of it is backed up on a flash drive."

"I'll pay for the damage."

"Thanks—it's not that much. My laptops are pretty simple. It's the software and the plug-in that are costly."

We sat in silence for a moment while Grant ran to the cop cars on Alameda.

"Has anything like this every happened to you before?" he asked.

"Incredibly, it has. You?"

"Never, and I'm thinking I should start charging hazard pay for field work. Are we going to tell your friend what we discovered?"

"I think we better tell someone," I said. "I don't much care for this getting shot at."

Chapter 10

"Not necessarily."

The remark turned my head around. More than that, it reminded me that my good but linear brain might be over its parietal bone on this one.

Grant and I were sitting in the kitchen of the deli. There were two officers out front, and one had climbed the fence and was watching the back door, which was open. It was a little past eleven PM, and the rain had stopped, leaving a fresh feel to the chill night and an oil-like slickness on the asphalt under the dumpster. I was sitting on the stainless steel table, Grant was leaning against the sink, and Banko was in the office.

We had come to the deli in a squad car. I'm not ordinarily claustrophobic, but I felt that way now, sandwiched between Grant to my right and Banko to my left, with two officers up front. It was odd to feel more in danger when I was "safe" than when I was actually in danger. I was the proverbial fish in a barrel.

On the way to the deli, there had been a lot of chatter on Grant's radio and on the squad car radio, and I didn't really listen to any of it. Grant wanted to know about the security guards who were on duty. When he interrupted a message to text something, I'm sure he was asking them to run a check on Banko. He wanted to know as soon as the ballistics team on-site knew anything about the direction and nature of the bullet fired at me. He also asked the officer watching the martial arts school to report in.

I don't know what he had learned or hoped to learn from all those inquiries. There was cross talk and broken reception and code, and ultimately he would boil it down for me. When we reached the deli, I apologized to the driver for the muddy seat; he gave me some perfunctory response, which I immediately forgot, and we went inside. I scrubbed myself in the bathroom and put on a change of clothes. Banko, less messy, rinsed off his shirt, wrung it out, and put it back on. He was more concerned about the computer, which was frozen. I left him alone, with the space heater on and the door closed.

I made coffee, gave Grant his—annoyed that I knew how he liked it, since that just reinforced the bond I was trying to put in my rearview mirror—and sat on the table with mine. There was a distinct unreality to the world right now. A man dying on top of me, culture shock from the martial arts school, embracing the idea of etheric readings, being abducted, redneck guards, another shooting, the rain, the park, and other things. All of that under my belt, yet here I was in the most familiar surroundings in my life—as though all of the rest of it could have been a dream. When I first got to Nashville, I'd spent a few nights at the deli while I familiarized myself with how it worked. I slept on this very table. Often, I wept with fear at the unfamiliarity of my new life and woke with renewed determination to succeed in it. The nightmares I had on those nights were exactly like the reality I had just come through: raw and messy. But those were the key words: I always *came through it.*

Buffered by the police, I believed I would come through this. And not just because of the police. Which brings me to the comment that turned my head around.

Grant was debriefing me. Slowly, gently, patiently, but progressively. He wanted me to come clean about Banko Juarez and why we were there.

I did. I told him about the etheric readings. He made notes in his pad, without expression. He once told me that police heard some pretty nutty things and could never dismiss any of it— not because they believed it, but because they wanted crazy people to keep talking. The more they said, the better the chance the officer might find some nuggets of truth. I hated the idea that Grant was humoring me, but I went along with it. Being shot at trumps righteous indignation any day or night.

While we were speaking, Detective Bean arrived. If she was annoyed to see Grant here, she didn't show it. I had assumed this was "her" case. Maybe parts of it were, like the Chinese angle. Maybe other parts weren't, like the "me" angle. She entered with her iPad held casually before her, as though it was a hand puppet ready to go on-stage. It was like an electronic vacuum, sucking in evidence. Maybe Banko wasn't nuts after all. How was this so very different from his ant-hair gadget?

Grant returned to the security guards, asking for any details I could remember about exactly what was said. He didn't break his stride when Bean walked in. I looked at her, saw her stony ex-pression, didn't bother smiling, just kept on going with what I knew about Banko's computer. When I was finished, silence fell like a sack of flour. Except for the low, vibrating hum of the motor that powered the freezer, it was quiet. Grant was in front of me, Bean was behind me, and I could see him looking at her and knew she was looking at him. I felt like a badminton net before the game.

"Anything from the field?" Grant asked.

She must have shaken her head because Grant looked down at his notes. "Given the M.O., I'm inclined to think we've got the same shooter."

That was when a familiar, hot butterscotch voice said, "Not necessarily."

I saw Grant look up as I turned. Bean turned back; with her iPad, and soon we were all staring as FBI Agent Lawrence Bowe-Pitt entered the room. He approached like the *Hindenburg* nosing its way into Lakehurst in the newsreel images: slowly, purposefully, with me as a mooring mast. I absently sipped coffee, which added an unseemly sound to his arrival, like someone *greptzing* at a funeral.

"Listening to the scanners again?" Grant asked.

"Believe it or not, Detective, the FBI has its own sources of information," Bowe-Pitt replied.

"Which we would ask you again to share," Bean said, "only we don't think that would do any good."

"Right," Grant added. "Because our job is preventing homicides, while your job is ripping out hate groups by the roots—only you need bodies to find those roots."

In just a few seconds I went from feeling like a net to feeling like bait. I didn't much care for either of them. I saw Bowe-Pitt's smoky eyes looking down at me from that sequoia height of his. There was a look of not quite compassion but not quite disinterest there.

"You've had an eventful night," he said to me.

"We're in the middle of an interview," Grant said. "If you wouldn't mind waiting."

The big man folded his hands in front of himself and stood where he was. The NPD was going to have to settle for his cooperation, not his departure. I wondered what Grant would do. I was a net again.

Grant turned the interview over to Bean and went to chat with Banko. He ever so slightly shoulder-butted Bowe-Pitt as he walked past. The agent towered a head higher, so it was more like an upper-arm butt. If Bowe-Pitt noticed, or cared, he didn't show it.

Bean and I went back to the security guards. I told her as much as I could recall of the conversation. I said that, the exact words notwithstanding, there was nothing overtly hostile in the exchange. I wasn't sure they would have known we were there if they hadn't come out to smoke. I couldn't say whether the smoking was a cover to get a closer look. Talking it out, I realized I didn't know very much for a fact—everything was an impression, my own edginess imparting intent that may not have been there.

When I was finished, Bean looked over at Bowe-Pitt. "Since we all want to get the shooter or shooters, would you care to share anything you have?"

"Gladly, but I don't 'have' anything," Bowe-Pitt said.

"You said you don't necessarily think we have the same gunmen—"

"I said nothing about what I *think*," Bowe-Pitt said. "I was merely noting that we can't assume it was the same shooter. It might be. He or she missed Ms. Katz through the reflective glass window of the deli, tried again in the park, and missed in the rain. Or it might be a copycat. The first killer was aiming for, and got, Mr. Chan. Now someone is looking to take out Ms. Katz or perhaps Mr. Juarez. The news reported the caliber and make of the rounds fired at the deli. Do you know how many hunters hereabout use 180-gr. Nosler E-Tip?"

"No," Bean said. "How many?"

"One thousand, two hundred boxes, fifty count, in the last year," he replied.

I heard that damn freezer motor again. It was like a maid pretending not to notice when the lord and lady were feuding.

"So we know very little, and that is frustrating to me," Bowe-Pitt said. Despite the words, his voice showed no agitation, nor did his eyes display heat or hostility.

"Us too," Bean replied. She looked at me. "Thanks for your help. Are you going to be all right?"

That question seemed like it was woman to woman. I appreciated it. She made her way around Bowe-Pitt with a little more finesse than her predecessor had exercised. The dirigible-man approached me.

"Who is the man in the office?"

I told him. He heard the information without comment. He stopped when he was a human mountain standing before me like Mount Sinai.

"There is this way of doing things," he said, cocking his head toward the office where the two detectives were huddled outside the door, "and then there is another way."

"I don't follow."

"The traditional way of solving crime is fact, fact, fact, thesis. I'm not sure that is the best way to go. You have been shot at or near. I also learned you were abducted. You are the only one who has been at the epicenter of these events. You're a survivor, and I'm big on intuition. What does your gut tell you is going on?"

His approach took me by surprise. "How do you know I'm a survivor?"

"I read up on you," he said.

"What, like secret files?"

"Good lord, we don't have a lot of time for those. It's not like the old days. No, I looked at newspaper articles. There was a mention of your divorce in the *New York Post*—"

"Phil wanted to hurt me by hurting my business," I added bitterly.

"—and the interviews you gave to the press when you moved here. They all told me you have some steel in you. The individual I see before me is a little beaten but still unbowed."

"So what do I feel?" I asked, sipping coffee. "I feel like the pieces don't fit."

"How so? Don't think about it—just talk."

"We've got a martial arts school with possible gang-affiliated enemies up north, white supremacists, three oddly nosey guards, a Jew who has been here fourteen months and never had hate directed at her, and random acts of violence that seem to have come from nowhere. I don't think they're all related. There are too many players."

"And those are just among the ones we've been looking at," Bowe-Pitt agreed.

That was one oddly worded statement. Extrapolating from what Bowe-Pitt had said earlier, it suggested that there could be more suspects he wasn't yet looking at *and* there could be more he didn't even know about.

"Got any leads?" I asked, surprised by my boldness.

"No."

"Thoughts?" I asked, refining my word search.

"A few," he replied.

"Anything you'd like to share?"

"Only by asking you this in the name of being thorough," he said. "What is the nature of the tension between you and Detective Daniels?"

Of course, my first reaction was to throw the coffee mug at him—which I refrained from doing. My second reaction was to override the first. My third reaction was to wonder exactly what bothered me about the question: the invasion of my most private privacy or the implication that Grant had gone from being a bad choice for me to being homicidal. My fourth reaction, the one that stuck, was curiosity about why he was asking.

"It's a relationship that is over," I said. Before he asked, I said, "I ended it."

"Do you know if he's seeing anyone else?"

"I don't, and if he is I don't remember him ever talking in his sleep or calling out the name of an ex at an inopportune moment," I added. "Even so, any mountain we climbed did not rise high enough for him to want to kill me."

He smiled just a little at that. I hoped I'd covered everything in my reply.

I had to admit, once I'd calmed down, that I respected his asking a tough question. I hoped it wasn't intramural squabbling but a sincere effort to eliminate a remotely possible link.

"Since you've been down here, five dead bodies have ended up on your doorstep—two literally," he said. "Except for mass murderers, serial killers, and the Civil War, that's a Nashville record. Any thoughts on that?"

"If I believed in karma, I'd blame it on my or someone else's past life. Just rotten coincidence." Strangely, that question didn't bother me. It was one I'd asked myself.

Grant walked in with his colleague. "May I talk to you, Gwen? In the office?"

I don't know why I looked at Bowe-Pitt—other than that he was ginormous and in the way—but I did. His face was impassive again. I moved around him, slid by Detective Bean, and joined Grant and Banko in the office. Seated in my squeaky chair, Banko looked totally harried, worse than before. His left hand and forearm were draped protectively across his laptop. I lay a comforting hand on his shoulder, and he flinched. Grant knew from experience that the door was pretty porous, so he didn't bother to close it.

"I'd really like to take Mr. Juarez's computer for a forensic analysis," he said to me.

"You haven't told me *why*—" Banko insisted, his voice shriller than usual, more desperate.

"I have," Grant said to him. "I've also told you that you can cooperate or I can get a court order."

"And I'll say it again: I have proprietary software in that machine, and you're not getting it," Banko said. "There is nothing in the computer that will be helpful to you."

"Sonic recordings of a gunshot *are* useful in cases like this," Grant replied.

"They are not sounds; they are etheric energy," Banko said.

"Whatever they are, they may be helpful."

That was pretty flimsy, and we all knew it. Grant probably wanted to rule out Banko as a possible accomplice, and I could certainly see both sides. I could also see Grant's damp, muddy trench coat and the muck on his cheeks and chin. I was not unaware of how he had protected me in the park. I owed him this one.

"How about this, Detective," I suggested. "We do the whole thing right here. Your tech guy comes in, checks out the computer while Mr. Juarez watches."

"Checks out the etheric file," Banko said. "Just the file."

"Just the file," I agreed.

Grant looked at me with hooded, disapproving eyes. He knew I knew what he wanted. I indicated for him to back off by widening *my* eyes. I let him know, with a look, that I would handle this.

"How do I know I can trust them?" Banko asked. "Someone could load the software into a flash drive and I'd be screwed."

"Okay then," I said. "What if we do it in the open, in the dining area, where we can all see everything that's going on? No flash drives. No plug-ins. Just a police person at the keyboard under your direction."

"We don't even know if anything *can* be retrieved from the laptop," Banko said. "It's been through a lot."

"That's true too," I said, "in which case this'll be a very brief project."

"When would they do this?" Banko asked. "I wasn't planning on being here past tomorrow morning."

"Tonight," I suggested, my eyes drifting to Grant. "Now."

Grant and Bean both recoiled a little, but Banko seemed a little better with that.

"What about compensation for my time?" Banko asked. If he had nothing else, the man had *baitsim*.

"I'll kick in an hour, Detective Daniels will pay the other half," I said. "That's three hundred bucks total."

I glanced at Grant and Bean. They looked like

they'd just got a snootful of bad milk. I'd explain later that I knew something Grant did not: when a person is getting paid for something, they let their guard down. If Banko had nothing to hide, he would, for money, give the forensics person some room to work. If he were concealing something, he'd still hover like a hummingbird.

Unless I ran interference. I didn't think the NPD was buying the etheric energy angle at all. I was, though. Banko had said in the park that we had a match. My game plan was to get him to do that comparison work, off his flash drive, on my office computer while Grant's tech person monkeyed around with Banko's machine. I would promise to watch Banko's computer while he checked the lines.

"So," I said. "We're all very tired—at least, *I* am. And some of us could probably use a little dinner. I'll take care of that, and I'm guessing that Mr. Juarez can still leave tomorrow—assuming we have an arrangement here, as my garment industry *mishpochas* used to say."

Banko pretended to consider the offer, then accepted with a nod.

Grant said, "We do."

"Great," I said. "Mr. Juarez, why don't you set up where you're comfortable?"

Bean went into the dining area to get a tech person over ASAP. I stepped back into the hall to allow Banko and his computer egress. As I did, I could see an admiring smirk on Bowe-Pitt's lips. I wouldn't say that we had a "thing" going, but we understood one another and admired each other's technique.

I was guessing that he wouldn't be going anywhere during this phase of the investigation. Which was fine with me. If someone was gunning for Nashville's favorite deli owner, the more law I had around me, the better.

Chapter 11

I was a little unnerved having Buddha in my kitchen.

I finally realized that was who Agent Bowe-Pitt reminded me of. Not the teacher of the Noble Truths, but the quiet soul who realized that all things must come to an end. He was going to let us all run ragged until the only one left standing was the killer or killers. And run we did.

I liked the NPD tech guy, thirtysomething Richard Richards. Liked him a lot. He was a civilian who worked for the department's Information and Technology Division, cute and possibly single. He was not part of any criminal investigation unit but was judged to be the best data-recovery expert in the city. He had grown up in a trailer without electricity and, from his earliest childhood, had learned how to "borrow" juice from others. He started by replicating Benjamin Franklin's kite-with-a-key experiment—

which resulted in electrocuting a mouse in a cage—when he was just seven years old.

"I was trying to jump-start a TV I found in the junkyard," he told me, while he set himself up in front of the computer. "I didn't understand about wall sockets or generators or how it all worked, but I learned. Second-degree burns from small transformers, from car batteries and jumper cables, are a great teacher."

He had a backwoods manner that put Banko at ease: his big blue eyes and blond hair and clean-scrubbed face, without a hint of midnight stubble, made him seem innocent, trustable. He looked at the grime-encrusted keyboard with a twisted mouth and a sigh.

"This looks like a Titans football via Minnesota," he said.

Not being a sports fan, I guessed that meant a game played in snowy muck.

I suggested that Banko eat his dinner, which I'd left in the office—as he and I had discussed while I prepared the platter. We were working on a little butcher-block table near the oven, away from Agent Bowe-Pitt.

I said quietly, "You want to show the detectives, the FBI, that you are onto something with etheric readings, right?"

"Right."

"Then you should go and get the results while they're all here and looking to break the case," I told him. "These guys are fishing. They need to bring *something* actionable back to the precinct, right?"

"Right."

"Okay," I said. "So give them a match. I'll watch your laptop while you find out which of those squiggly lines from the park was at the deli when Ken Chan was killed."

He seemed dubious. Whether it was the proprietary software or something else, I couldn't be sure.

"You'll let me know if he gets the thing up and running?" he asked.

"The instant I see a welcome screen through the mire."

He looked along the corridor at the two detectives, who were standing in the open front door, waiting for their guy.

"I'll do it," Banko said. "But you've *got* to watch them."

"Like Shylock with his accountant."

Banko made a strangely puzzled face at that as I finished making dinner and Richards entered the deli.

Richards was seated at the counter, and I hovered over him so that Banko would see me every time he leaned back in the chair and looked over. I kept Grant and Bean away, and Bowe-Pitt had remained in the kitchen, reading texts and e-mails. The new arrival used a paper napkin to gently, almost lovingly wipe the screen of shmutz while he waited to see if it would boot. That was when he told me about his background and I told him about mine. I noticed that he wasn't wearing a ring. Actually, I didn't notice: I looked. It didn't mean he wasn't married or even straight, but it was good to know.

Then the computer spoke in a high, grinding voice.

"That's not good," he said. "Gunk in the gears."

He typed fast, and a moment later white letters scrolled swiftly down a black screen.

"What's that?"

"A diagnostic program I created," he said. "I use it to poke around in the hardware, look for areas of compromise."

"How did you upload—?"

"I didn't," he said. "I'm downloading whatever raw data is in there, however compromised and garbled." He tapped the cell phone he wore on the left side of his belt, away from the office. "The wonders of Wi-Fi."

I felt a little guilty. I must have looked it.

"Don't worry," he said, crossing his arms as he waited. There was a tattoo of a kite on his right bicep. "Detective Bean gave me my parameters. I'm turning a scrupulously blind eye toward installed programs."

It was strange to hear words like "scrupulously" riding that clucky backwoods accent to my ear. I know. It was stereotypical of me, biased, and all the things I hate that people do to Jews. But I consider myself immune since I'm the first to remark, at least to myself, on the antithetical behavior of my own people, like when one of my *schnorrer* cousins picks up a check or I get through a dinner with my childhood JAP friend Marci without her whining nasally even once.

"Is this the data that's going to your phone?" I asked, nodding at the screen.

"No. It's showing me the pathways to the data and jumping over sections that were compromised in the fall. I'm not going to learn anything from—"

He stopped. So did the computer—or so it seemed. There was a long stretch of black before the white letters started up again.

"That's weird," he said. "I already passed the file I wasn't supposed to look at."

"Meaning?

"That black space? That's a file that no one's supposed to see."

My conscience pinged harder. The not-seen file was what I personally wanted to see.

"What do I do?" he asked.

"Did it download to your phone?"

"A black-line copy would have," he said. "It will look like the censored sections in government documents."

"Can you remove the black lines?"

"Possibly," he said. "It's easier if I use this computer."

"How long will that take?"

"A couple of hours," he said.

"I should've put Ambien in the gefilte fish."

He looked up at me. "Say again?"

"Nothing. We only have it for a few minutes."

"Then I'll have to work with the download," he said. "I'm pretty good at this. I should be able to get something from it."

Those last two words came out like "frawmt." It was adorable.

That was how this was going to be done. Richards finished the download, the computer choked on its own diagnostic, and he called the detectives over. Banko emerged as well, looking wary. I was angry at him: after all that, he *was* hiding something. Maybe it was none of my business; maybe it was porn; maybe it was politically incorrect blog posts—who knows? But he could have told us if we were wasting our time. And saved me a hundred and fifty bucks, which I was thinking of getting back from him with the edge of a meat cleaver, if necessary.

"This mule's dead," Richards said when everyone had gathered round.

I was watching my now-nemesis. He seemed relieved. Unfortunately, since he wasn't supposed to know we'd run into his firewall, I couldn't very well challenge him on it. Not unless my life depended on it—which it might.

Grant and Bean nodded gravely. They had known exactly what he was doing. Richards shut down the computer and closed the lid.

"Sorry, Mr. Juarez."

"It's okay," he said. "I was expecting as much. In the meantime, I want to tell you all something."

Agent Bowe-Pitt wandered over as Banko was speaking.

"I have a flash drive that has my etheric line readings on it," he said and shot a look at Grant. "*Only* my etheric readings. As I explained earlier, those are energy radiances that come from individuals without their being aware of it, sort of like radio waves. Anyway, one of the individuals Ms. Katz and I encountered tonight was in the deli this morning, before Mr. Chan was shot."

"One of the guards—or the man walking the dog?" Grant asked.

That stopped Banko like a custard pie in the face. "I don't—I'm not sure," he sputtered.

In Banko's defense, that hadn't occurred to me either. Not that this let them off the hook, but we were so fixated on the guards we didn't bother to notice anything about the other man. I made a face and looked at Grant.

"Is there some way to find out if the dog walker did eat here that morning?" I asked. "He could have been eyeballing me for someone."

"Anyone with a telescopic nightscope could have eyeballed you," Grant said.

"Not with the glow coming from that computer screen," Agent Bowe-Pitt pointed out. He was standing behind the two detectives, a wall of devil's advocacy. "That would have washed everything else out. The proximity of one man at two shootings—whoever that man was among the etheric lines—would seem to merit attention."

Grant doesn't like sharing authority. He likes

being humiliated even less. I saw the flesh redden around his collar, threatening to reliquefy the mud splatters.

"We will be checking everyone out, of course," Grant said. "Thanks very much for your input."

"You are very welcome."

Bowe-Pitt's politeness was worse than his initial comment. Grant left after counting out one hundred and fifty dollars and tossing it on the counter. Detective Bean looked like she wanted to say something to Agent Bowe-Pitt, but didn't. Richard Richards rolled his lips together, slipped from the stool, and extended his hand to me.

"I had a really pleasant experience here," he said.

"Thank you, Mr. Richards."

"You are very welcome, Ms. Katz," he said with the kind of southern grace and sincerity that accomplished what Grant's huffing did not: it showed Bowe-Pitt there was a better way to handle people. Then again, Grant's reaction was apparently exactly what Bowe-Pitt had hoped to get. Otherwise he wouldn't have done what he did.

I thought of a couple of things I wanted to say, like "Stop by for lunch" or "Call me when you know something" or "Take me home with you." Only the first would have been remotely appropriate, though not under the circumstances.

Richards left, and Banko tucked his computer back in the shower curtain.

"I have to put that back in the bathroom," he explained.

"Yeah, I know."

"Can I walk to the hotel from here? Is it far?"

"Not very." I told him the directions. He thanked me for an exciting night, said he probably wouldn't see me again, then thanked me for dinner. I had to stop myself, *really* rein myself in to keep from asking him to pay for it, the secretive little *shmegege*.

Then it was Agent Bowe-Pitt's turn to go. It was not like saying farewell to the Scarecrow. I won't say I liked him less than the others, but I sure didn't respect him as much as I had.

"Grant's a good detective," I said.

"I have heard that said."

"What I mean is, he didn't deserve that kick in the teeth."

"I knew what you meant, and I knew you would feel that way. But I don't like sloppy work. Detective Daniels was being belligerent—because he's frustrated, I think, by more than this case. I don't have time for that. You, as a possible target, should reject that even more vehemently. Your friend Mr. Richards—he was good. He pulled off that data heist without arousing suspicion."

I stood there like lox on a hook. I replayed everything he said, and he was right. Grant let his emotions take charge; so did I in my response to Agent Bowe-Pitt.

I turned away, saw the spot where Ken Chan

had died, looked away again at the base of a stool. I wasn't expecting Bowe-Pitt to say anything consoling, but it would have been nice. Instead, he said, "I am going over to the NPD to see what he comes up with."

"How do you know he'll work on it tonight?" I asked without turning.

"I watched him while he watched the 'diagnostic.' He loves what he does. He'll work through the night. He couldn't wait to get back, despite potential distractions."

A brocha, did this guy miss nothing?

"I will notify you if there are additional precautions to be taken," Bowe-Pitt said, as he headed for the front door.

"Such as?"

"Mr. Juarez knows how we are protecting you," Bowe-Pitt said. "So do Detectives Daniels and Bean—"

"Oh, come *on!*"

Bowe-Pitt stopped and faced me with that Wailing Wall of a torso. He spoke softly so the officer at the door wouldn't hear. "Do you know if Detective Daniels has ever been abusive to a woman or a prisoner?"

"I do not, but abuse isn't—"

"Murder? It's not as far off as you might imagine. The brain gets knotted up, it doesn't function rationally. If it doesn't get to unwind, it snaps. Do you know if Detective Bean is sweet on her colleague? Do you know if she has ever killed anyone in the line of duty? Do you know if she was put on psychological furlough?"

"Was she?"

"It doesn't matter. You don't know the answer, so you can't rule anything out. You don't know me, though you can assume the first thing Detective Daniels did was check me out before he accepted me on premises with you. That much I *do* know. I also know that Detective Daniels did not check to make sure the officers on guard have no connection with the university. I did that. You don't want to be guarded by someone who may have been a part of a radical campus group or might be a member of the SSS." He came closer. "Details in an investigation, Ms. Katz, are like the ingredients in a pie or omelet. You might think the milk is bad, but, in fact, it could be a pinch of sugar instead of salt or a bloody spot in an egg yolk."

That was disgusting, but he was right. Dammit: the guy was a pro.

"I will make sure the officers front and back have been briefed of the potential danger, but just so you know, they are being watched by someone I called in from my bureau. Don't go wild if you see him."

"What do you mean?"

As he left, Bowe-Pitt said, "He's a man walking a little dachshund."

Chapter 12

I didn't sleep so well.

The air mattress leaked and was flat within an hour. I slept on the floppy vinyl and swore I could feel every edge of every tile. My cats, who had gone from the office to a place behind the counter, decided to show their anxiety by rubbing my face or crossing my belly just after I started to doze. I finally had to get up and put them back in the office with the door closed, where they occasionally mewed their discontent.

More than that, though, my brain kept me awake. I kept pulling "what ifs . . ." from Bowe-Pitt's parting comment. So he had a guy in the park, which meant he had been following me from some point: probably after the abduction, since that would have justified calling in extra eyes.

He could have parked, got out with the pooch, kept an eye on things. That would mean it wasn't his etheric line that was in the deli. That would make it one of the security guards. Which didn't mean they were the ones behind the shooting—but it sure put them in the running. My question was, what did the other FBI guy do after the shot was fired? Did he see a flash? Did he run toward it? I didn't even know what direction it had come from. I didn't know if Grant had any idea.

Worst of all, when I thought about it, that *pisher* Bowe-Pitt hadn't told Grant that the guy in the park was his man. I guess if he even remotely suspected Grant of being a crazy person that made sense; still, it seemed a little counterproductive. The NPD was going to spend a certain number of person hours looking for a guy who didn't live in the neighborhood.

That tactic—or game playing, which it partly was—troubled me. Along with what we didn't know, this situation was more frightening than anything I had experienced in any of my criminal escapades down here.

So I was up, with coffee made—and half consumed—by the time the staff arrived for work. I gave Luke stacks of menus to pass out on the street to let people know we were open for takeout. The gunfire in the park had made the morning news but not the target, so other than what-in-the-Lord's-name-is-happening-to-this-city lamentations from Thom, no one knew I was the possible target.

The police didn't let reporters in, so Candy Sommerton and Robert Reid and other media linchpins who put in a personal appearance did not get in. I ignored their calls. It was only day-old soup, and they were still keeping it warm.

The caller who surprised me, and whom I told Luke to bring in, was the short, round-faced woman I had seen at the martial arts school the day before. She was now dressed in a more traditionally western black skirt, black blouse, and black jacket. There was a small black-and-white photograph of Ken Chan in a black plastic brooch she wore on her left lapel, over her heart.

She approached with the same delicate steps as the day before. I had been cutting pastrami on the slicer when she arrived. I wiped my greasy hands on my apron, took it off out of respect for her mourning, and walked over to greet her. She stopped a few paces from me, her hands at her sides.

"I am May Wong, called Auntie May," she said.

"Aha! Ken Chan used your phone to call me."

"Possibly," she said. "We had the same type of phone. He must have called you before we realized we had switched them by accident," she said. "That is not important, and it is not why I am here, Ms. Katz. Last night, when you did not return to the school, I realized that I had made you feel unwelcome. I am here to apologize. That was not my intention."

I wanted to believe she was sincere. Yet for all I knew I was abducted by others at her school—possibly by Auntie May herself.

"Would you care to sit down, have some orange juice or tea?"

"Coffee, black, would be nice," she admitted. "I did not rest very well. Nor you, it seems." Her eyes settled on the kitchen. I hadn't bothered to move the deflated mattress.

"I had a restless time. Tell me, Auntie May, do you work at the school?"

"I am an accountant," she said. "I do their books."

"Really? I was an accountant once, sort of," I said. "At least, that's one of my two useless degrees. Did you have an office in New York?"

"Yes, on East Broadway."

"I knew a broker who lived there, off Grand Street. Sammo Biau. Ever hear of him?"

"No," she replied, with a pinched, embarrassed smile. "I didn't move in those speculative circles. I enjoy the orderliness of books and ledgers."

"I prefer the orderliness of recipes," I replied. "Less chance of ruining someone's life or retirement."

She didn't seem to be listening. She sat at the table where I'd placed the coffee. Thom looked at us both with surprise. Without realizing it, my groggy brain had put the cups at the same table where I'd been seated with Ken Chan. I decided not to move and said so in my return look at Thom. There was no reason to make things even more uncomfortable for Auntie May.

"May I ask where my nephew died?"

I froze with the cup at my lips. Thom made an I-told-you-so face.

"We were on the floor," I said. I set the cup down, rose slowly, and stood on the spot. It was at the farthest reach from the table, where my head was lying, about five feet away. She looked at it a moment, then put her steepled hands together beneath her chin, bowed to it very slightly, and began drinking the coffee I had poured.

"I wish to invite you personally to the wake," May said.

"I appreciate that, and I would like to honor your nephew, but I have a feeling I'd be intruding."

"A loss such as this needs to be filled, and not by hate or blame. My family knows this, and I believe you will fill it with something positive."

That was an enlightened view, I had to admit. It was nothing like my upbringing, where funerals brought out the absolutely most covetous, uncensored worst in everyone. Still, somebody in this clan or one affiliated with it had abducted me. If I went, I'd feel like I was walking around with a target on my chest.

On the other hand, if the persons who kidnapped me were there, I might actually get a sense of who they are.

Did I want to reenter that situation after the caller told me to stay out?

"You did not know my nephew before yesterday?" Auntie May asked.

She wasn't just making conversation; she was

probing. All of a sudden the invite seemed like a pretense. The tone and questions of my abductor came rushing back. Like her, Auntie May was asking for information simply by inflection, not with a "how?" or "why?" or "did you?" The tone chilled the small of my back.

"Sadly, I did not."

"Sadly, you say? Did you like him?"

"Very much," I said to her.

She smiled thinly. "Women did."

"I'm not surprised. He had a sweetness, honesty, gentleness." I was making myself sad, eulogizing him like that. I stopped. "Anyway, we hit it off. I size people up pretty quickly, and he struck me as a good man. Certainly his deeds speak for themselves."

"They do," she added, looking into her cup as she drank. "They do indeed."

Was she being sarcastic? Strangely, it sounded that way. "When and where should I be?" I asked. "For the wake."

"Come back to the school any time today," she said.

"Are you absolutely sure? I won't feel slighted, I understand—"

"Please. Come."

I looked at her and smiled a little smile. She could be inviting me to my own funeral, for all I knew. But if they wanted to work some kind of *meshugass,* they could just as easily do it here. Plus, if the guarded looks of my staff were any indication, the police would know who to question if I disappeared—again.

"I'll be there," I assured her.

She drank more coffee, and we sat in awkward silence for a moment. It was uncomfortable for me, at least; Auntie May was pretty inscrutable.

"There was a shooting in Hadley Park last night," she said at last. "You have heard of this?"

"I have," I answered guardedly.

"Might they be related?"

"I don't know."

She was holding the cup near her face, her eyes on the rim. Then those small, black-marble eyes snapped to me. There seemed to be another question on her lips. Her mouth made the smallest kissing motion several times in succession. Then the lips, and she, relaxed. But not the mood. That stayed tense.

The strained silence returned. So did her little smile. I was less interested in whether Auntie May knew I was being evasive than in why she wanted to know. There was only one way to find out.

"Why are you asking me about the park?" I inquired. She couldn't—shouldn't—have known I was there.

"The two attacks seemed to have similarities," she replied. "It is a reasonable assumption that they are related. Our family, our school, is obviously interested in knowing if it might be the same person who killed our *sifu.*"

"I understand," I told her.

"It is not to be vengeful," she assured me. "That would go against the *sifu*'s teaching."

"Great teachers are like that," I said. "Peaceful." Though, in fact, the only two one who came to mind were Socrates and Jesus. And things didn't end well for them either. It was a good argument for militancy. "Look, I promise to let you know anything that the police are inclined to let *me* know."

"That is most kind," she replied. She set the cup in the saucer and stood. "I have taken up too much of your time. You are preparing to reopen?"

"Only takeout," I said. "We have had experience with people coming in and gawking."

"Thank you for that," Auntie May said. "You bring dignity to this tragedy. I will see you later, then?"

"Yes."

The woman smiled again, nodded at Thomasina, who was staring straight at us from behind the cash register, then made her way to the door.

"That was like watching Peter and the maid," my religious manager said.

"I'm an Old Testament girl, remember? Peter and who?"

"The maid. Peter's mantra to her and the others: deny that he knew Jesus."

"Oh yeah. I'm familiar with *that* story."

Thom's hands came down flat and hard on the countertop. "You were at the park, weren't you?"

"Why do you say that?"

"Because you skipped around it when she asked, and you didn't deny it when I just asked. So you were there?"

I nodded like a little girl.

"Meaning somebody took a shot at *you*."

"Possibly," I said.

"Possibly? A rifle was used here, a rifle was used there, according to the news—"

"Okay, conceivably."

"*Lawsy*, my soul whispered to me that was the case, but I didn't want to hear it, *I did not want to hear!*" Thom said that with her tendency toward the dramatic, teeing up with an exclamation whose meaning still wasn't clear to me. I assumed it was some kind of variation of "Lordy," but it never seemed the right moment to ask. And this wasn't it. Her face was an iron mask of disapproval.

"I'm being more careful now, and both the NPD and the FBI are covering my *tush*."

"You gonna tell them you're going to the Chinese wake?"

"I don't think I'll have to," I said. "The FBI has been following me."

"That's a relief," Thom said. "Glad somebody got some common sense."

"Are we ready to open?" I asked, knowing we weren't.

"I will be. You *know* I will be."

I don't know how many employers would put up with the kind of back talk I got from Thom— only I know it came from a place of love and deep concern. I knew that, and the love and concern were mutual.

People started lining up at eight, and while Luke maintained the line, A.J. and Raylene took the orders. They ran them to Thom, who brought them to me and Newt in the kitchen. I caught glimpses of the customers as they came in to pay and walked away with their orders. Most were regulars, and I appreciated their support. A few were clearly rubberneckers who wanted to lay eyes on the death spot. One was a crime blogger, Marcel Carney, whom I recognized from when our bread man had died out back. He came in, shot a video while pretending to talk on his phone, and left just as I flung a wet washcloth at a surprised Thom with instructions to scrub the counter. I came within a few inches of hitting him.

Unlike most days, when there's a breakfast and lunch rush with a lull between, the flow of customers was constant. I didn't get to check e-mails or answer the phone. Part of the crush of patrons was due to a slight backup caused by having to make everything to go. It takes a little more time to wrap and bag food items than it does to slap them on a plate. We ran out of to-go packing several times, which necessitated digging into the supplies in the basement for more paper, more bags, more Styrofoam containers. Some of them still had a smiling caricature of my uncle on them.

By late afternoon I was kaput. As soon as Dani

came in I checked out. Thom handed me my messages, I went to my office, shut the door, shut the phone, and lay back in my chair. A surprisingly uninterrupted hour-long nap took the hard edge off my exhaustion, after which I helped with the busier-than-normal late-afternoon crowd, which included Candy Sommerton buying bagels and trying to convince Thomasina to let her see me. I was surprised the blond newscaster did not leave wearing the *schmear* in an unseemly spot. To my outsider's eyes and politically incorrect brain, it was more than just Thom looking out for me. It was the War Between the States being played out in reverse. A century and a half ago, what I was witnessing would have been unthinkable. Thom would be beaten to or nearly to death.

Which brings me to a few words about our bagels.

After the death of our McCoy's Bakery bread delivery man, whose firm had decent bagels—thanks to Uncle Murray sharing his recipe—I decided it was time to home-grow our own. Not just because our customers deserve the best I can give them, but because working on Wall Street taught me the value of individual enterprise: job creation. If banks are the backbone, then small business is the circulatory system of our economy. I found a baker who had been laid off by McCoy's, Louis Radich, and set him up with an oven in a former machine shop he picked up at foreclosure. He was free to bake for whoever he wanted as long as he made my bagels first—by which he was paying off the interest-free loan for the forty-thousand-dollar stone-hearth deck oven. I bring this up because it's necessary to put some perspective on my own not exactly paranoia, but guardedness.

Blacks and other minorities have made stunning progress. Except for dwellers on the radical fringe, people go out of their way *not* to lash out at them. Muslims get multi-faith rallies to decry Islamophobia. Illegal immigrants get federal mandates affirming their rights. Gays and the transgendered get legislative protection. Single mothers with five kids from different fathers get state assistance. Blacks, Latinos, Native Americans, and every blend or subdivision of those groups have grassroots advocacy in towns and cities and on college campuses.

Not me and mine. I'm not *kvetching*, mind you. It's been that way for millennia. We're raised to be on guard. Which brings me back to Louis. His wife convinced him that "I"—meaning Jews—had enough money and that he should charge me a delivery fee for the small amount of gas he was using to come to the deli during his daily rounds. He broached the subject. I told him, fine, but then I'd charge him interest on the forty-thousand-dollar loan. That came out to way more than the gas. He withdrew his request, embarrassed that he had made it. His wife e-mailed that I wasn't being fair. I didn't respond.

My point being, while Thom is and feels free

to express herself, I was raised to expect every act to boomerang—if not by the nature of the act then by the fact that I am a Jew. True or not, that paranoia is in the air, in the genes, in my soul. And that fear was playing out in my brain even as the evidence failed to provide any actionable information. Who was angry at *me:* the SSS or the Chinese? I didn't have enough information to make that call. It's worse when you're a woman because, added to that, you're wondering if someone like Banko is a perv or Detective Bean is sweet on Grant and angry at me for maltreating him or whether Agent Bowe-Pitt is an anti-Semite or a misogynist or both, even though he appeared to dislike me, Bean, and Grant equally. I spend so much time working out ancillary issues that there is less time to focus with clarity on the main problem.

Like: would I be walking into some kind of viper den at the wake? Or, more important, would I be walking out again?

I didn't know. All I knew for sure was that I had to go if for no other reason than to get hard data or firm impressions to push aside the feelings of bigotry and oppression. I dressed in black slacks and a black sweater, which were all I'd brought with me, since black is the default going-out color of New York women. I weathered Thom's disapproving eyeballs as I headed for the door.

I didn't get out clean, though. As I was leaving,

my office phone rang. Thom answered it at the counter extension.

"Do you want to talk to a Richard Richards?" she asked.

I hurried back to my office.

Chapter 13

I took the call in my office, glad to hear from Richards because he and his manner and his voice relaxed me, and curious to hear what he had to say.

"I didn't clear this with the detectives, who are out, so I hope you'll keep this between us," he said.

That was sweet. Either that or I was really hungry for a kind soul. Or, more likely, both. "Not a breath will escape," I assured him.

And then he said, "Your friend Mr. Juarez is a pimp."

I remember, when I was about five years old, my father and I built a snow man in Washington Square Park. It was about six feet tall, and while my father was putting the head on top, I was on my knees behind it, reinforcing the section where the torso met the base. Suddenly, the big snowball that made up the bottom collapsed and the entire figure fell on me. I was startled at the time, though I knew I shouldn't be: we had piled too much snow too high on too little base.

That was how I felt now. I had put an awful lot of weight on a foundation that was obviously shaky. I was startled for about a second—and then everything fell into place.

"There was enough on his laptop for me to go online and see that someone operates a series of websites across the country offering escort services on an 'in-call' basis, meaning at local apartments or motels," Richards said. "There were exotic first names and references to 'roses' in the data. Roses are the buzzword for dollars. Oh, and before you ask how I know that, it's my job," he added quickly. "It was easy to connect several of the websites to his laptop."

"So Banko goes around the country, stays in places where he's already renting rooms, and does his little experiments on the side."

"Apparently."

I didn't think the etheric research was a fake. Given how quickly he jumped at the opportunity of legitimizing his studies—with the very group, law enforcement, that would be keen to shut down his other activities—I guessed it was more of a passion for him than the actual big-earnings work he did.

I asked, "Is there enough to file charges, do you think?"

"Probably not," he said. "I did conduct what was, in effect, an unlawful search. And I understand that he did leave town late this morning. Didn't he contact you?"

"I don't think—" and then I told Richards to hold on. Thom had answered the phone throughout the busy day, written down my messages on those little pink pads, and handed them to me. I looked at the thin stack on my desk. One of them was from Banko. No message, other than to call him back. He left his cell number. "Yeah, he did."

"If anything, this is probably a matter for your agent friend to follow up on," Richards said. "I'm sure the gentleman is out of our jurisdiction by now, if not out of the state."

"Right."

"There also isn't anything, as far as I can tell, that has to do with Mr. Juarez's energy research, other than the blocked software," Richards said. "He seemed to be cooperating on that front, so I didn't look into it."

"What about the shooter in the park?"

Richards was silent and then made a *hmm* sound.

"Is that a 'yes, but I can't tell you?'" I asked.

"I should really let Detective Daniels or Detective Bean handle that."

"Meaning there *is* something."

"A point of origin," he said reluctantly. "But I really, really shouldn't be talking about that."

"I understand," I said. And I did. If I didn't like the man I'd have pressed him. Instead, I'd press Grant.

"I just wanted you to be aware, in case you are in touch again, that Mr. Juarez has had some shady dealings with which you might not want to be associated."

"I really appreciate that. And I hope to see you again under happier circumstances."

The sentence hung in the air like a high pop fly. We both watched it, wondering if it would land foul or fair.

"I'm sure we will," Richards replied, which as far as I was concerned was the equivalent of having a beer spilled in your lap.

"Great," I replied ambivalently as the ball game suddenly became about my wet blue jeans.

I couldn't hang up fast enough, and I even wiped my hands on the sides of my pants. They were sweaty and felt unclean. My brain blanked on everything we had discussed, except for that last painful exchange. I struggled to regroup.

Right, I thought. *I've got to return Banko's call.*

I looked at the computer clock. I decided to call Banko when I got back from the wake. I needed to think about what I would say to him, and I couldn't do that given where my head was now. In a strange way, knowing the truth strengthened my belief that *he* believed in the etheric studies he was doing. The man made sure I knew nothing about his income-producing work, lest my opinion color all else. The funny thing was, I didn't have a problem with his pimpery. A woman should be allowed to do what she wants with her body. In fact, maybe these ladies were smarter than me. I'd done some pretty stupid, destructive things in that area and come away totally empty-handed.

I decided to drive to the school. Given what had happened the day before, it seemed to make more sense to have a couple of tons of metal between me and a potential kidnapper or gunman.

The trip took just a few minutes, even in early rush hour traffic. That was the thing about Nashville that I would never get used to. Even the exit from the city was a relatively brief spurt instead of the flood it was in New York. It was almost cute.

The police car was still parked around the corner. I pulled up behind it. The same officer was on duty. I was surprised by the availability of parking until I saw the bicycles chained behind the school. I wondered if it was fitness or economy or both that was responsible. Then I noticed a banner on one that went off like fireworks in my brain: it was emblazoned with a tiger atop the letters TSU.

Tennessee State University.

Oy.

As I passed the window I saw about two dozen people inside. That wasn't the only change from the previous day. The mirrors on the side of the school had been covered with bed sheets. There was a gong standing outside the door to the left. A young man dressed in black stood beside it, outside the door. He was a stern-looking fellow, more like a bodyguard than an usher. Beyond him I could see the casket of Ken Chan. It rested on ornate blocks that raised the bottom to about eighteen inches off the ground; the foot of the coffin faced the window. There, at the foot, was a table overflowing with offerings of food. At the head were little tables adorned with framed photographs of Sifu Chan. Only a few people wore the brooches with photographs that Aunt May had been wearing. I assumed they were family members. They were the only ones who were sitting, all of them on stools that were low to the ground.

I glanced over at the young man. He wore an expression as iron-hard as the gong. I tried not to take it personally. The man was in mourning.

"Hello," I said. "Is there—I've never been to a wake like this. Is there anything I need to know?"

"About the wake or what is expected of mourners?"

"I guess—both?"

He said, "To begin with, take off your shoes before entering."

"All right." As I began removing them, I saw where the others were lined up just inside the door.

"The mirrors are covered because we believe that if you see the dead in a mirror, the death will be repeated on another member of the family," he said. "The gong, placed to the left, informs passers-by that a male has died."

It was like the Jewish custom of sitting shiva;

in that case, the mirrors were soaped, though that was to discourage inappropriate vanity. Outside the home was a different object—a bowl to wash the dirt of the graveyard from one's hands. It was interesting how similar-but-different elements showed up in unrelated cultures.

"One thing more," he said. "Do not crawl to the casket."

I looked past him. Several people were on their knees beside it; I hadn't realized they'd crawled there.

"That is only for relatives who are not part of the immediate family."

"Thank you," I said. "Am I permitted to kneel?"

"You are permitted, though it is not expected unless you were a student."

My ten-minute acquaintance with the deceased did not qualify me as anything other than a fellow New Yorker who was briefly his caterer. I walked inside, as the young man held the door. Only once before had I experienced a sensation of standing out so completely—and it was not when I went to a show at the Apollo in Harlem during my college days. There, at least, I was with another Jew, even though he was Ethiopian. It was when I went to a Buddhist meditation center in Chinatown. The experience was like one of those Inspector Clouseau movies in which, as quiet as you tried to be, your shoes squeaked or your breathing was wheezy or the fabric of your blouse made rustling sounds. It was so quiet inside that every sound seemed sharply magnified.

There were glances in my direction, but no one stared. While most of the mourners were Asian, several were not. They were young, students most likely, ranging in age from around fourteen to nineteen. They were wearing their traditional uniforms, black with white frog buttons and rollback cuffs. The solemnity of the occasion was heightened by the dress; to say I looked out of place is to state the apparent.

I found Aunt May among the understandably sad—even sour-looking—family members. I would have felt a little better if she had done more than glance at me then glance away. No acknowledgment. Maybe there was an aspect of Chinese mourning that I didn't understand. It made me feel totally adrift. I stopped when I reached the casket—which was closed—and I stood for a while with my head bowed and my eyes shut. I thought of the brief moment we shared and it made me grin. With the smile still on my lips I turned to May. From where I was standing I could see a young woman with a small girl at her side. The girl was four or five and as petite a little lady as I'd ever seen. The widow and daughter, I presumed; she had her mother's sad eyes and high, proud forehead. I felt I should go over and say something, but without any kind of sign from Auntie May, I didn't know if I should.

Which is ridiculous, I reminded myself. *You don't know who the target was.*

Nonetheless, he was killed in my deli. I was about to go back and ask my friend at the door when the young woman rose and walked in my direction. She was tiny, about four-ten, with the most delicate-looking features I had ever seen. Her daughter stayed behind, sitting on her stool and looking at the casket as if the sadness and weight of the planet were on her straight little shoulders.

Maybe they are, I thought. I remember being that old and thinking that the dress I couldn't have or the friend who suddenly, inexplicably wouldn't talk to me was a tragedy. How does a little girl react when something truly is catastrophic?

The woman stopped in front of me.

"You are Gwen Katz?"

I told her I was.

"I am Maggie Chan," she said in a grieved, respectful whisper. "Thank you for coming. May I speak with you privately?"

That was a surprise. I'm sure it showed in my expression. "Of course," I said.

Auntie May regarded her through slightly narrowed eyes. "Are you sure you are up for this, niece?"

"I am," she replied.

There appeared to be a "moment" that was way over my head. Though the meaning was elusive, the tension was very real.

Maggie turned toward the office in the back of the school, along the same side as the covered mirrors. It was literally not much more than a closet, about half the size of my office. And this one had mine beat in terms of clutter. On the facing wall were trophies with martial arts belts and caps draped over them; on the wall above hung certificates and framed and lopsided photographs of people in martial arts uniforms, along with candids fixed to the wall with push-pins. There were newspaper articles, though nothing that seemed older than three months. A sign of the times: they were printouts from newspaper websites. To the right were shelves filled with VHS cassettes and DVDs of movies and what looked like training videos; a small cathode ray TV and various connected players were stacked precipitously on a stool. On the left side was a desk with a laptop, a phone, various hand exercisers worn from use and stained from bodily oils, and sundry knives and guns that, I assumed, were used in training but kept here for safety. Among the items was a small, framed photo of Maggie and their daughter. There was no photo of the deceased. Those had apparently been moved to the shrine.

Maggie shut the flimsy wooden door behind me. I felt a flash of concern at all the weaponry. I wondered if she knew kung fu. I tried not to worry for my safety. Why would Auntie May have lured me into a trap?

To stuff my body into that casket with Ken Chan, I thought. *Maybe bury me without a trace.*

Maggie did not offer me the only seat, a straight-backed wooden chair. I didn't take it personally. If someone sat in it, there wouldn't be room for anyone else inside the office. She stood with her back to the door. I faced her.

"I am sorry that you are involved in this situation," she said.

"I'm sorry it happened," I said.

"Thank you. But you don't know the entirety of it."

The feeling of being out of place evaporated. I was suddenly right at home, my catcher's mitt on, ready to receive hardball information about a crime. It was amazing how a slight tilt toward the familiar could take body, mind, and soul with it.

I waited expectantly as Maggie's eyes went to the photo on the desk, lingered, then came back to me.

"This was supposed to be a joyous day, when the school comes together for promotions," she said. "Instead we are in mourning."

"I'm so sorry." I was, though I was beginning to wish I hadn't come. This was additional agita I didn't need.

"We grieve as a family and as a closely bound community. A school is like a church or a veterans' organization or a trade union. We are one."

I nodded. Inwardly, I cursed her considered Eastern manner and my own wild Western impatience. I remembered my mother playing her own vocal devil's advocate as she walked around the house. So did my grandmother. At least I was keeping those contrarian voices on the inside.

"Ms. Katz, how did the *sifu* seem to you?"

"Very, very happy," I said.

"Do you have any idea why?"

"I assumed it was the ceremony—but it could have been just being down here, alive. It could have been meeting a fellow New Yorker. It could have been all of the above. All I know is that he put me at ease."

She smiled very, very faintly. "He was like that with most people. Was he wearing his wedding ring?"

That was a surprising question. I had to think about that. "I don't know," I said. "Was there any reason he wouldn't have been wearing it?"

"He always took it off for class lest someone be hurt or one of the punching bags torn. In skilled hands it can be—what do you call them? The hard fittings placed on fingers to hit people?"

"Brass knuckles," I said, sounding like I'd walked out of a John Garfield movie.

"Yes, brass knuckles. Sifu often forgot to put it back on. He usually kept it here." She pointed to the arm on a trophy.

"I understand. But the ring is on his finger now, right?"

"Yes."

"Forgive my asking, but what made you ask?"

"Vanity," she said. "I liked to know that he was thinking of me when he was out."

I wondered if maybe he didn't take it off to fight but to conceal the fact that he was married. It wasn't like men had never done that before. It was the international sign of "cad." I wondered if Mrs. Chan had wondered that too. Or maybe there was another reason. Who knew what confused thinking lurked in the minds of men?

The woman took a long breath with her hands in front of her, slightly cupped, as though they were riding the outside of an inflating balloon. It was like everything was ritualized. Or, more likely, it was a way of life I didn't understand. I began to see why outsiders—and some insiders—thought Orthodox Jews were incomprehensible and a little scary. What looked like eccentricities and tics were vital ritual neatly and unobtrusively threaded into the fabric of their lives.

"Do you see the article on the wall?" she asked. She pointed to the printout.

"Yes."

"Three months ago the *sifu* judged a kung fu competition in Memphis," she said softly. "His vote broke a tie, and the trophy was awarded to a bright young martial artist named Chingmy Mui. Though she attends a school in Memphis, she has visited here many times. The runner-up in that contest was a young man named Donnie Li from a school in Knoxville. It is not a part of our teaching to take defeat as a humiliation but as a lesson that we need to improve. Yet there are many who view a loss to a woman as a loss of face. Before the day was out, the Li family had begun to spread a rumor that my husband was involved in a relationship with Ms. Mui."

"May I ask . . . was it true?"

She did not reply.

"You know it was the Li family who spread the rumor?" I asked.

"There was no one else," she said. "After the competition Ms. Mui stopped coming to visit. She was not in contact with any of our students or with the *sifu* for those three months. And then her name appeared on the list of attendees for tonight's belt promotion. The *sifu* was very, very happy." The woman was silent for a long moment, staring at her hands, which were folded across her waist. "But then she came last night to pray at the shrine. Ms. Mui is three months pregnant."

The first word in my head was *gevalt*. The pregnancy was not incriminating, of course, but the timing, her withdrawal, and the rumors sure didn't make it look good. It would also explain Maggie's interest in the ring. When you're insecure about a relationship, even the smallest gestures matter.

"Ms. Chan, I hate to ask this, but would someone have tried to kill your husband over this relationship? Not just the family, but perhaps a jealous rival?"

"I do not know. I truly do not know."

"Let me rephrase that," I said. "Would it be a loss of face the way it happened—I mean, hillbilly style, with a rifle from a distance, instead of face-to-face?"

"The younger generation does not always understand such things," she said. "And to have challenged him in a fight would have been pointless."

"He was that good?"

"No. He would not have fought. He was a man of peace."

Translation: that would mean dishonor for whoever came here and beat him into *tsibilis*. Better if it were anonymous. Of course, all of this was still speculation. Whoever killed him might still have been aiming at me.

"I wish I had more to offer," I said. "I feel pretty helpless—and I don't like to feel that way."

"There is no need." She looked at me. It seemed as though she wished to say something else and decided against it. "Ms. Katz, I very much appreciate your coming here and also taking the time to talk to me. I needed to meet the person with whom our beloved *sifu* spent his last moments."

"I can only say that I was glad to have met him," I told the woman. "Actually, that's not all I can say. He saved my life. That's a pretty major thing. I want to thank you, thank everyone, for whatever training he had or code he lived by. I hope that thought will sustain you, just a little."

"It is who he was," she answered sadly.

She looked at the clippings and certificates. I didn't know if that meant I was dismissed, but I took the opportunity to leave.

"Wait a moment," she said.

I hesitated in the doorway.

"May I have your cell phone?"

I was perplexed but passed the phone over to her. She studied it for a moment, then tapped some buttons and handed it back.

"My telephone number. If you should ever need it."

"Thanks," I said, not sure why I would but appreciating the gesture.

Once again, though I moved as quietly as I could, it seemed as though I was creating a racket. Not just the floor squeaked; the door also did. I swear, my ankles did. I walked past the family, bowed my head to Auntie May, who dipped hers back; I turned once again and bowed to the casket, then made my loud, cacophonous way to the front door, which the young man opened for me after I put on my shoes.

Dammit, but the open street and the fresh air felt good. I felt as if there were a dog on my tail as I walked briskly to the corner and my car. It was all in my head, I know, the self-consciousness of the Jew in an unusually strange setting.

As I left, something occurred to me.

Maybe Chan *wasn't* looking at the napkin holder right before he was shot. Maybe that look of distraction wasn't about focusing on someone outside the window. Or about a splash of mustard that may have caught his eye. Or a dent. Perhaps, for some reason, he was thinking back. Or ahead.

What was it, Sifu? I asked him, frustrated and confused. *What was going on at that moment?*

It was a wispy, elusive thought that nagged me for the rest of the night.

Chapter 14

It was nearly nine PM when I phoned Banko Juarez. I got back to the deli, said goodnight to the policemen fore and aft, fed the cats, then sliced some Hebrew National salami, slapped it on a hard roll with Guldens, and went to my office. I took off my shoes and put a pair of very tired feet on the desk.

As I had expected, the etheric cleanser told me he'd gone to Kentucky on—I kid you not—the last train to Clarksville. He said he had appointments in Lexington. I did not doubt that. But he did not want to discuss his whereabouts, which I also understood. He really, really, *really* wanted to talk about his etheric findings.

"I couldn't wait for you to call back," he enthused. "I discovered something amazing about the two lines!"

"Do tell." Until the words came from my mouth, I didn't realize I was in *that* kind of mood, sarcastic bordering on cynical. What Banko hadn't told me about himself undermined my faith in his authenticity. I wasn't be angry at him for making money from women who sold their bodies; a lot of people have agents or brokers, in which case he and I had some stuff in common. But liars?

"I was busy comparing the lines from your restaurant with the lines from the park when I noticed something peculiar," he went on quickly. "There were none that were the same."

"Is that good or bad?" I asked over a mouthful of ham and bread and rolling my eyes and wanting to hang up. But I didn't. When he was done I was going to give him both barrels.

"Neither. It's fascinating. They were similar but not exact. So I started tinkering with the software to bring up—do you know what fractals are?"

"Sort of, but not really," I said.

"Well—it's not that important. I amplified different sections of my readings to look for similarities and discrepancies, and I made a real breakthrough. The lines of those two have a familial overlap, almost like a genetic map!"

"And that's important because . . . ?"

"It's like a remote DNA test!"

"But only of living people, correct? Because dead people don't have energy."

"That's right."

"So how does that help us? It seems to me you've just undermined your own research:

whoever was in the park may not have been in the deli."

"Yes, it could have been a sibling or a son or daughter—"

"Who knows nothing about these crimes," I pointed out.

"Right. But it proves that my investigations *work* on a more sophisticated level than I imagined!"

This was without a doubt a stunning waste of my time. Though, as I looked around the office, I really didn't have much else to do. Other than going over Thom's bundled receipts and checking her tally, there was only computer solitaire in my future. I didn't want to reveal that we had stolen data from his computer, but I decided to play this yarn ball out.

"Explain fractals," I said.

"What?"

"You brought them up. What are they?"

"It's a structure in life or math that has a pattern that, at whatever scale you examine it, reflects the shape of that object," he told me. "It's like seeing increasingly smaller patterns in a leaf that may not be identical to the entire leaf but are still clearly identifiable as a part of that leaf."

I wouldn't bet the deed to the deli, but that definition sounded right.

"So then, would one hooker be a fractal of a stable?" I asked. Yes, I said it with a heavy dose of irritation. But I don't like men who lie to me.

Call it scar tissue from my marriage, feminist ire, or just my own predilection for truth-telling, however blunt and tactless that may be at times.

There was a brief hesitation. "No," he said. "I'm not sure what mathematical definition would apply."

"Perhaps a triangle, if the guy was really generous?"

More silence. "What am I missing here?" Banko asked.

"You? Nothing. I'm the one who's missing something."

"What would that be?"

"A piece of the story," I told him. "Your story."

"I still don't follow."

I had to dance around it to protect my source. "I get the feeling that you were not at that hotel by chance."

"I told you why I was there," he said.

"The readings, right. You're devoted to high-energy situations."

"Exactly."

The silence that followed was more useful to Banko than to me. I just looked around the office, waiting. He was obviously thinking, no doubt about whether to fess up. I had a deeper concern, one that had been knocking around the back of my mind.

"I still don't understand what you're talking about," he said disappointingly.

Banko was either very stupid or very stupid, depending on which kind of stupid I went with.

If he were truly missing my point, that was naive stupid. If he were still trying to perpetuate a lie, that was just plain stupid.

"I'm talking about hookers and your involvement with them," I said. "What's your involvement with them, beyond etheric readings?"

"Is that really any of your business?" he asked.

"It is if you were the target," I said. "There was a guy who looked like you sitting at the counter when Mr. Chan was shot. Through the window, someone might have mistaken him for you. How do I know it wasn't you being shot at in the park?"

"That's ridiculous," he said. "Who would want to shoot me?"

"Exactly what I'm trying to find out," I said. "Are you involved in any kind of business that would inspire a hit?"

"Only if someone knew I'd recorded the energies of a killer or his accomplice," Banko said thoughtfully.

"*Loch in kup,*" I said. "What about a pimp turf war?"

This time Banko did not respond with silence but with a gasp.

"Didn't think I knew, eh?" I said.

"Actually, you're scaring me," Banko said. "I have absolutely no idea what you're talking about!"

I was no longer staring at the *tchotchkes* on my desk. My tired brain was replaying what Banko had just said—not only the words but the tone. He sounded as earnest as a Chasid on Yom Kippur.

"You have nothing to do with prostitutes?" I asked.

"What a question! Not that it's anyone's business, but I never hire them."

"How about anything else?"

"Like *what?*"

"Like—when I got to the hotel the concierge asked if I was one of your prospects." It was an improbable lie, and he probably knew it. All of the ladies I saw were younger, taller, better built, and undoubtedly veterans of far more tangos than I. They also probably earned more, which irked me more than the other stuff. But that was the only thing I could think to tell him.

"It was probably a joke," he said. Then, realizing what he'd said, he added, "I mean, you don't look like an escort."

He said "escort," not "hooker." I wondered if he knew the lingo. I did, from the time I checked the websites visited by my former husband.

"Thanks. That's what all my out-call clients say."

He didn't bite. Not even a *huh?* Maybe he was really, really practiced at covering his illicit tracks. Or else he had no idea what I was talking about.

"Back to the more important matter," he veered back quickly to his own geeked-out agenda, "it looks like one of the three guards or the dog walker had a relative who ate at your deli. A shot was fired after both encounters. That seems important. We should let the police know what I've discovered."

"Sure. I'll handle that," I said.

"Tell them to call me if they have any questions," he said.

"I will."

We hung up, and I was more perplexed than when I'd called. Would a man with something to hide offer to answer questions from the police? No, I told myself. Even if his etheric device worked on some level, it couldn't be that difficult to pick Banko up in Kentucky for soliciting, or whatever nice word they used to describe pimping, and extradite him to Tennessee.

Tennessee.

The word echoed in my brain. My eyes drifted across suddenly unfamiliar surroundings. *I am in Tennessee.* What the hell was I doing here? And being held in protective custody no less. With people dying around me.

Just go. Pack up the cats and leave.

Just. Go.

"Uncle Murray—this is a lot more than I was expecting," I said to a fading, cracking Polaroid photo tacked to the bulletin board. It showed my father, my uncle, and me during one of our fishing trips in Montauk when I was a kid. "Why is this happening? It isn't like I'm not working hard."

I saw the round face, receding hairline, and frozen smile looking back at me. How did he do it? How was he always happy? Because he had a real passion—music and songwriting? *No,* I told myself. *It was because he had priorities.* He didn't keep one eye on the business and one eye on potential relationships and one eye on music and one eye on questions like these. His priority? Being happy.

I bit off a bit of ham, and it sat in my mouth, unchewed. I wanted to cry. I wanted to *talk* to someone and there was no one. I ate the mouthful, sat back, and stared at the ceiling and answered the office phone when it sang without looking to see who was calling.

"Hello."

"Gwen Katz?"

"Yes." It was an unfamiliar voice with a slight southern sparkle.

"My name is Chingmy Mui. Sifu Chan was my teacher."

"I know who you are," I said.

"I thought you might. May I speak with you?"

"Sure." I was apparently the clearinghouse for all things Ken Chan.

"Face-to-face, I mean."

That set me on my guard. "Why?"

"I want to meet you."

"Where are you?"

"I'm at the police cordon, out front," she said. "They will not let me in."

That was a surprise—*another* surprise. "You're alone, right?"

"Yes."

"Forgive me for being cautious, but I had some difficulty with some of your friends or enemies yesterday—I'm not sure which."

"I am very sorry for that. May I come in?"

"Sure," I said. "I'll meet you at the front door."

I hung up and got up and tried to perk up. I couldn't. My bare feet dragging, I found a nugget of glass that had been blown from the window the other day. That woke me. I pulled it from my heel and tossed it in Thom's wastebasket. I went to the door and looked out.

No one was there. Not even the police officer.

My brain went to Defcon One before my body did. Fortunately, my body deferred to my brain. I dropped facedown as a bullet charged into the counter behind me. Some survival instinct instructed me to roll from the door, and I did, backward, protected as a second bullet hit the jamb. By the time a third bullet clipped the floor, I had rolled into the diner, behind the plywood, where I was safe.

The shooting stopped. I heard footsteps coming through the restaurant from the back door and others from down the street. The front-door cop was in the door, her gun drawn, talking into her radio and looking up at the rooftops across the street. The back-door officer dropped to my side.

"Are you hit?" he asked.

I did a push-up to get off my chest. Nothing

seemed weak, numb, or tingly. With the officer's firm, supportive hands on my arms, I tucked my knees in and rose on them. There was no blood on me or the floor.

"I think I'm okay."

"Do you need medical attention?"

"No," I assured him.

"All right, back to the office," he instructed, as he helped me to my bare feet and now very wobbly legs.

I went. While I waited for the cavalry, I checked the phone log. The call had come from a public phone. I was sure the police could pinpoint it. I was equally sure they'd find it was somewhere away from any kind of surveillance. I was somewhat sure that it wasn't from Chingmy Mui at all. Now that I thought about it, nothing she had said indicated any prior knowledge of my abduction. I offered all the information.

The triumvirs arrived separately. Detective Bean was first on the scene by about a minute, Grant was second, and Agent Bowe-Pitt was third. They all made their way in via the back door so as not to contaminate the crime scene.

Bean strode past the office door, saw me sitting on the edge of the desk as she passed, and doubled back. She asked what had happened and I told her. I asked where the officer was who should have been at the front door.

"Called away by a cry for help around the corner," Bean said. "Radioed it in. Said she would not be letting the front door out of her sight."

And she hadn't, apparently.

Grant walked in just as I had started telling my story. When we were done, Bean left, Grant stayed.

"You've got dirt on your blouse," he said.

"*Shmutz.*"

He smiled. "That's right."

I saw my unfinished ham on a roll, took a bite, chewed slowly.

"Can I get you anything?" he asked.

"Yeah. The person who keeps shooting at me. Did you find anything in the credit card receipts?"

"I can't really talk about that," he said.

I made a face. When we were intimate, he told me everything. He knew he could trust me; who would I tell? This was his way of punishing and controlling me. But I did realize something just then. "I guess we can assume it's me they were shooting at, right? There were no Chinese here."

"Unless Ms. Mui was actually out there somewhere," Grant pointed out.

"Then why shoot at the store?"

"To keep you inside," he said. "This could be some kind of a vendetta against her, against the school, against Mr. Chan. We've spoken to the family. That's a complex situation over there at the school."

Dammit, that was true. The officer *did* hear a cry for help. And there might be a pay phone around the corner—I usually went the other way and couldn't say for sure. Though why would someone use that if they owned a cell phone . . . unless they didn't want someone to know they were placing the call.

"No one on the rooftop," I heard over Grant's radio. "Looks like another two-hander. No obvious leave-behinds."

"Copy that," he replied.

There was a two-story building across the way, one that stretched nearly the full length of the block. Because of a setback in the rear, it was easy to pull over a trash can or milk carton and get up to the roof of the first level, then take the external fire stairs on the sides to finish the ascent. Or, as the officer had suggested, it was accessible via a two-hander: one person boosts another up. They had clearly cleaned up after themselves as well, again.

Grant fixed those strong eyes on me. "We can move you somewhere a little more secure," he said. "A hotel or even a hospital room."

"I'll be okay, I guess, as long as I stay out of the doorway," I said. "I wonder, though, why whoever it is keeps shooting? Why not a homemade bomb or something?"

"Easier to trace, especially if it doesn't work," Grant said. "And then there's collateral damage."

"Like Ken Chan wasn't?"

"That was out of the shooter's control," he said. "I'm going to have a talk with the officers, make sure they don't get pulled away for any reason. You sure you're all right?"

"As well as a gal with a bull's-eye on her back can be."

He smiled, then left. Thank God he was being professional Grant and not personal Grant. I needed the room and freedom to *plotz* inside. I shut the door, slid into the chair, and stared at my ham on a hard roll. I had no desire to finish it. I had no desire to move. A fear of my own mortality, of possible lurking death, caused my hands to start shaking on the armrests. I gripped the worn leather tighter.

And lost it.

I bit my right forearm so no one would hear me, really shoved that sucker in my mouth. *What was happening? How had I come to this place in my life?*

The tears were like a squall, hard but short-lived. My crying spells were usually like that. I poured out the pity, then got my act together to do what needed to be done. One thing I had always been able to do was muster a good offense to serve as my defense.

Someone was at the other end of that rifle. Someone who might be related to a person who had been in my deli two mornings ago. Whether or not I knew names or noticed what people were wearing or carrying, I saw every face in the place. About eighty percent of those people were known from credit cards. The police were interviewing them. The other twenty percent were in my head—buried by the shooting.

I had an idea. It might not be a good one, but it was better than sitting here. I went to the safe and got a couple hundred dollars in cash.

Before Grant left, I asked him for a ride. I figured there was no harm: if he saw me go out, on foot, or hail a cab, he would only follow me anyway.

"Where are you going?" he asked.

"To the Page One," I said.

"*Why?*"

I trampled his horrified expression by heading for the door and replying, "To search for clues."

Chapter 15

Grant did not come inside with me. It would scare the clientele who might recognize him, and it wouldn't do his reputation a world of good. Though, I thought, it might loosen him up a little. One of his problems is he was always wound tight. Yes, always.

My friend was behind the counter, the big-bosomed, up-selling concierge. She gave a sly grin when she saw me.

"Another reading?"

That surprised me. Banko said—

Banko lied, I realized.

"No," I replied. "You mentioned a hypnotist?"

"Dr. Cagliostro."

"You're kidding."

"Everything about me is quite real and very, very serious," she said, pushing her chest forward a little.

Cagliostro was the nom de guerre of eighteenth-century Italian occultist Giuseppe Balsamo. It had the right sound for the job, I'd give him that. "Can you call up to see if he has an opening?"

She let the smile flower. "Your name again?"

"Gwen Katz."

"Just a minute," she said and placed the call. She did not take her eyes from me the entire time. I looked away, noticed I was in the cross-hairs of a security camera, wondered if she was sending one of those images to Cagliostro's room since she hadn't said anything after hello and giving my name. About a half minute later she hung up and told me to go to room 826.

I went up and stopped at 816 en route. I listened. I didn't hear anyone inside and decided to call. I punched in the number and listened again. It did not ring inside. I hung up before Banko could answer.

All of which means nothing, I reasoned. *He could be out. He could be doing a reading.* I continued down the hall.

Dr. Cagliostro was not what I was expecting. For one thing, she was a woman. For another, she looked about ninety. Her skin was paler than that of the lady at the desk and she was as thin as a meaty skeleton. She wore sunglasses, but she was not blind. She was dressed in white slacks and a white blouse. She wore a red shawl and was barefoot. Her white hair was pulled into two tight braids. She had no makeup on, not even lipstick on her wide mouth.

"Come in," she said.

I entered, and she shut the door behind me.

The room was not like a hotel room: she obviously lived here and had dressed it to suit her Victorian tastes. It also smelled of cigar smoke. Hers, I guessed, from the box of Havanas on the dresser. There were ornate hooded lamps that cast low, yellow light and equally arch furniture. The drapes were heavy and red and looked like they were on loan from *The Phantom of the Opera*. What really caught my eye, though, were a pair of framed diplomas for Dr. Adrianna Cagliostro. One was a psychology degree from Columbia University, 1940. Another was a degree in psychiatry from Johns Hopkins.

As my *bubbe* used to say, *Klugheit iz besser fun frumkeit. Wisdom is better than sanctimony.*

"Sit there, please," the woman said in a voice like sandpaper. "Place two hundred dollars on the table beside it."

I counted out the twenties, then sat in a massive wing chair. She scooped the bills in a clawed hand and stuffed them into her breast pocket. She sat in an armchair beside the larger seat.

"What do you wish to know?" she asked.

"I own a deli in town," I said. "I want to see who was eating there two mornings ago. I want to see their faces again."

"Shut your eyes," she instructed.

I obliged. It wasn't that much darker with my lids closed since the largest lamp, beside the bed, was directly in front of me. But the ruddy amber light *was* relaxing. I was surprised, but not startled, when I heard her voice close to my ear.

"Were you sitting in your deli that morning?" she asked.

"In my office, yes."

"You are sitting in your office now," she said. "But not today—that morning. Look around. What was on your desk?"

"Unpaid bills and an inventory sheet," I said. "I was going to get to them later."

"Pick up the inventory sheet. What was on top?"

"Potatoes," I said. "We had a run on *latkes*. I needed them badly."

"Potatoes," she repeated. "Potatoes. Look at the writing, but don't speak."

I looked. I saw my scrawl on the legal pad.

"Look at the next item, but don't speak."

It was bread. That was always in the top five. Rye on top, white next, whole wheat after that. Then hard rolls.

"Next item," she said.

Kosher salt. I was going to get that at the grocery store.

"Next."

Napkins. People were slobs. Old ladies stole them to use at home. I always needed them.

"Next."

Coffee. That was partly my fault. I drank enough to float a . . . a matzo ball.

"*A matzo ball*," I said. In my head, I saw the one on Ken Chan's plate.

"Shhh," the woman said. "Next."

Milk. Eggs. Butter. The usual. I saw my customers slathering butter on pancakes, pouring milk in coffee . . .

"*They use so much,*" I murmured.

"Put the list down and look around the office again," she said.

I did. I saw the photos. The computer. The door—

"See the light as it was that morning."

I have no windows, but there was light in the hall. It was crisp. I had a big window, still. I smiled. The world had not yet gone wonky. The window was there, the diner was open for business.

"Get up and go to the dining room," she said. Her voice was a whisper, floating in my ear, in my head.

I got up, heard the squeak of the chair, walked into the diner. There were people—

"What do you see?" she asked. "You may speak now."

"Customers," I said. It was the damnedest thing: I could *see* them. I was there.

"Walk among them."

I did. I knew the deli so well that my brain effortlessly reconstructed it. I was sliding between the tables, slipping around chairs, looking at coffee cups to see if they were empty and plates to see if they were finished—and also at faces. The regulars, like our mail carrier Nicolette, bus driver Jackie and her girlfriend Leigh, who fixed my car, bank teller Edgar Ward, advertising exec Ron Plummer, and Brownie, Blondie,

and Big Red of the Repeat Returners Club.
There were tourists: you could always tell them
from the tour book, the iPads with maps, and
the cameras. Then there were the local newbies,
of which there were not very many. People
around here tended to have their favorite pit
stops and watering holes. They liked having a
waitstaff who knew how they wanted their eggs
or fries or coffee.

I tried to look at the new faces. I hadn't really
spoken to any of them, so I didn't really remember them. I reached the end of the dining area,
turned around, came back. I saw bodies—

"Relax. Slow down," the voice beside me said.

Right. I was pushing myself. *How did she know?*
Because she's done this before, *shmendrick*. Or
maybe my closed eyes were darting around, like
I was in some kind of mad REM sleep. Which
maybe I was.

I looked at the people sitting by the counter. I
didn't know two of the people. But one—one
had a sweatshirt I recognized. I'd seen the logo
on a bicycle parked behind Chan's school. TSU.

The guards were from TSU. But this wasn't a
guard. A student? That was no help. A lot of students ate at the deli.

Then I stopped short. I saw myself. And sitting
with me was Ken Chan. I think I moaned, but it
sounded far off.

"What's wrong?" the voice asked.

"I see someone who is about to die."

"What is he doing?"

"We're talking," I said. "Laughing."

I hesitated, looked around. Chan was reaching for the matzo ball. He forked it. He lifted it over his cell phone.

"You are smiling," the voice said. "Is there anything you need to see there?"

"Yes," I told her. "Just a moment."

Everything seemed to be in slow motion. I looked at him, at his eyes, at his hand, at the napkin holder. I heard his phone vibrate. He glanced at it, then looked away—to his right, my left. I saw the napkin holder just as I had seen it that morning. There was nothing to see in the polished aluminum, just a blur. He wasn't looking at that.

"His ring," I said. "He's looking at his wedding ring!"

Then the hand became blurred, and there was a flash. I gasped, and the hypnotist took my hands and shook them lightly and told me to come to her.

I did, at once. I actually felt myself pulling at those spindly fingers to get back. I opened my eyes and looked around the room. It seemed strange to be where I actually was and not where I had imagined myself to be. I can't say I had actually *remembered* myself being in the restaurant or I couldn't have seen myself. It was just an elaborate construct of memories that the woman had helped my brain pull together.

I thanked her and left the room quickly. I didn't even bother with Mr. Etheric Cleanser.

I wanted to tell Grant what I saw, not because I expected him to put any credence in it but because I needed to talk it out.

Grant was sitting in his car half a block from the hotel so as not to scare the clientele. I sat in the passenger's seat, sipped some of the coffee he had bought himself, and told him what I saw . . . what I thought. He was skeptical, as I expected. And he humored me, which I also expected. But that was okay. I needed a sounding board, not an advocate.

"Assuming there's anything to it, Gwen, what do you think it means?"

"Why would Ken Chan have been looking at his wedding ring?"

"Why would any man?"

"Maybe he felt blessed," I suggested. "Maybe he'd screwed up and had an affair and regretted it. Maybe he got Miss Mui pregnant and was wondering what to tell his wife? Maybe he was regretting that he was married to his wife and wished it were Chingmy's ring he was wearing."

"Maybe he suspected there was a contract on him and he was saying good-bye," Grant suggested.

I gave Grant a look. "He had given me a catering order. We were just talking happily about New York. He was about to eat one of my matzo balls. Why think that?"

"We recovered his phone," Grant said. "There was an unanswered call at that time. It was from"—he caught himself as he was about to confide in me, changed course, and said, "Someone we interviewed."

"Come on, Grant," I said. "Who? What's going on?"

"I can't tell you about the status of an investigation."

"Why? Do you trust me any less than you did a couple of months ago?"

"No," he said. "But what I did then was wrong."

He was right about being wrong, but it still ticked me off. "Grant, I'm being shot at. If not *at,* then around. I'd like to know if I'm the target!"

"I don't know." He had been looking down. Now he looked directly at me. "And going to see crazies like this one, like Mr. Juarez, isn't going to get you any closer to answers. You need to hunker down and stay out of sight as much as possible."

He was right about that too. But we both knew what was wrong about the cornerstone of that approach: me.

"If I were that kind of person we would never have met," I said. "I would be safe in the city I grew up in, a city I know. Over the last fourteen months I feel like I've always had a target on my forehead."

"That's not uncommon in public service jobs—"

"Because I'm Jewish," I told him. *God, what a lump this man could be.* "Just tell me if I've got the

SSS gunning for me or whether I'm just caught in the crossfire of some Chinese vendetta."

He was still looking at me. "I'll say this," he said after some consideration. "Both are potential triggers. Along with a third possibility."

"A what?"

"The officer who was shot a couple of weeks back, Sergeant Frank. The only people who knew where he was going were cops."

"The girl he was with? She knew—"

Grant shook his head. "First time there."

"Ow. But what does that have to do with me?"

"Agent Bowe-Pitt believes the SSS had a hand in that. Like any secret society, who knows where they are connected?"

I took a moment to process the information. Then I looked back at Grant, into his eyes. I could see that he wanted to share that with someone—his concern, his sadness, his disappointment. "Thank you for telling me that. I'm sorry."

"The PD's good folks, good apples," he said. "Sometimes one has a worm. It's bound to happen. I've been on edge leaving people at the deli—that's why I've had two there, why I or Detective Bean has been trying to keep an eye on the place. Why I followed you."

"I see. Thanks again. I'd like to go back there now, I think."

"You sure? Like I said, there are other places."

"I'll be okay," I assured him. "I'll sleep in the walk-in freezer."

For a moment he believed me. Then he snickered. "Just stay away from the doors, okay?"

"You don't have to remind me. And you don't need to sleep in your car."

He snickered again. Now that he'd let down his guard, he was clearly on edge, not just about me, I suspected, or even the possibility of a rogue cop, but the fact that someone was shooting up the city and he had been powerless so far to make any headway.

We drove the short way in silence. He saw me to the door, shut it behind me, and spoke to the officer out front—perhaps sizing him up? Grant was nothing if not a good cop. Ironically, I think he was doing his own version of taking an etheric reading.

I retired to the kitchen, heard Grant crunching through the alley to the fence to talk to the cop there. Both officers were new to me; Grant obviously wanted to make sure I wasn't being watched by the cops who had let a couple of bullets slip through and a gunman slip away. I shut the back door but did not bolt it. A minute later I heard Grant back around front, and I listened from my office as he talked to the forensics team that was just finishing up on the bullets and their trajectories. From his tone of voice—just the low, tense sound of it, not the words I couldn't hear—I knew he wasn't happy.

I shut the door and sat down to ponder the sketchy new information *I* had to work with: Chan's ring and his wistful gaze, which didn't seem to give me anything particularly helpful, especially if I wasn't actually remembering it but imaging how I remembered it—perhaps prompted, subconsciously, by my abductor asking me what else Chan could have been looking it. Then there was a student at the deli and at the school, which hardly counted as a novelty in either place. And finally we had a possible leak in the thin blue line, which could be dangerous to all concerned and might also be what Agent Bowe-Pitt was keeping *his* eye on.

A night of information, but, on the surface, a whole lotta *bubkes.*

The more I thought about it, though, there could be something to that cop thing. And there might be a way for me to do some checking.

A "crazy" way.

Chapter 16

When everyone had gone, I went to the refrigerator with scissors and cut several lengths of rope that were used to bind the lettuce cartons. I formed them into two makeshift leashes and tied them around my cats' waists.

We were going to go for a walk in the alley. And if not a walk, a drag. They were not outdoor cats and might not take kindly to going al fresco. But I needed to get out for a while and didn't want the cops calling Grant.

Southpaw and Mr. Wiggles did not want to leave my office. Specifically, they were tucked deep under my desk, where the confluence of wires and dust created an alien world of monstrous plant tendrils and puffy spores. I pulled them out like sphinxes being drawn through a cloud of desert sand. I rigged the little nooses around each, behind their forearms, and we went out the back door.

The officer, a veteran with skin pocked like gefilte fish, gave me a look.

"They're used to country living," I said preemptively. "They need to be outside."

He studied them as they were pulled past, then said, "They got no claws, ma'am."

"Yes, I know. I have a pen for them at home. Very safe. The noises and lights here scare them."

There was no traffic this late, and the fence blocked the lights from the surrounding shops. It wasn't kosher, we both knew it, but it wasn't as if I was under house arrest or anything.

"Would you like me to go with you?" he asked.

"No, I'm fine, really," I smiled as I pulled the cords harder to get the mewing babies up on their *farkakt* paws.

We made it around the corner to the alley; the wails of my two companions actually scared the bona fide alley cats. When we were out of sight, I picked them up and put them under my arms like a pair of footballs. I scurried to the street, leaned out slightly, and when the cop out front was looking the other way, I headed left.

The parking garage had my keys, and I had my driver's license and a credit card. I also had the two cats, but they would survive. The attendant knew me and waved—albeit with a strange look—as I hustled past with my two little lions.

A few minutes later I was outside Ken Chan's school. I pulled up in front. I got hit with a spotlight from the cop car as I approached. Then it snapped off. No one got out. The door to the school was closed, but there was a light on in the office. The wake was over; the casket was gone, though the shrine remained. Leaving the cats in the car, I rapped on the glass door.

I had a sense of reverse déjà vu as a head looked out from the office toward the front door: it was usually me on the other end of that action. It was Auntie May. She emerged, still wearing her mourning clothes and the same neutral expression I had seen at the wake.

She turned the key in the door and opened it slightly—just enough to talk, not enough for me to enter.

"Hi, Auntie May. I was hoping to talk to you or Ms. Chan."

She hesitated a moment, then stepped back to let me in. She locked the door behind her. "I am here alone, going through my nephew's papers. How may I help you?"

"I remembered something about—well, about that morning, and I wanted to ask you about it."

She extended an arm toward the back of the school.

"Is it customary for a wake to be so brief?" I asked.

"It was prudent," she replied. "There has been concern."

"About?"

She stopped and regarded me. "Murder requires a murderer. The students were watching to see who paid respects—and, more important, who did not."

"But Sifu Chan may not have been the target."

"Yet he was not without enemies," the woman replied, "and he is not without friends, friends who are looking for an excuse to attack those enemies. As I told you the other day, that is not our way."

We reached the chair by the shrine, Auntie May taking one seat and gesturing me to take the one to her right. I was aware of the smell of the flowers, which were more plentiful than they had been before. Roses, mostly, stacked in bunches before the shrine.

"What did you wish to ask?" Auntie May asked.

"Thinking back, I have this memory of Sifu Chan looking at his wedding ring moments before the attack. Is that something he did as a rule?"

"Look at it?"

"That's right."

"No," she said. "He did not wear his wedding ring—as a rule. We discourage wearing jewelry here. It can cause injury."

"Yes, Mrs. Chan told me that. What about at night? When he left here? Or in the morning, when he arrived."

Auntie May looked to her left, toward the shrine. "Your questions are very personal, Ms. Katz."

"I apologize. I need to know why his eyes on that ring stood out to me."

"Why are you asking that now? What didn't you tell us earlier?"

"The way he looked, what he looked at, was bothering me. It was the last thing he did before saving me—I wanted to understand. So I went to a hypnotist. She brought the memory out."

There was no need to say any more than that. Either she was going to answer or not. I waited. Things were as tense as they had been back at the deli. I didn't know if it was the culture clash, the topic, both, or something else. Such as secrets she didn't want to share. I had some ideas about what those might be, such as his relationship with Ms. Mui and the paternity of her child.

"I will tell you," Auntie May said after some consideration. It took nearly a minute before she drew a long breath and went on. "The man who was with you that morning was not Sifu Chan."

Okay: that was *not* on my short list of ideas. It wasn't even on the long list. I didn't even have a response. Although it also occurred to me, then, that during our office meeting "widow" Maggie had kept referring to the dead man not as her husband but as "the *sifu*." I thought it was some kind of show of respect, but now I understood why. Because he was, in fact, no more than "the *sifu*."

"The deceased was Lung Wong," she continued, "my real nephew, one who was with Sifu Chan in New York since the founding of the school in 1988. He posed as Sifu Chan so that the master could stay behind and root out the gang members who had infiltrated our school. It was important that word get back that the master was gone, for good. The real *sifu* needed to be free to act without endangering his family."

"A real ninja," I said.

"That is Japanese."

"Oh. Then—"

"A hidden snake," Auntie May said. "That is the animal identity he embodied."

"I see." I did, too. And now the questions my abductors asked made sense. Perhaps they were northern gang members who knew, or suspected, that Lung Wong was not Ken Chan. "So the question, then, is would anyone have wanted to kill Mr. Wong—the real one?"

"Several individuals," Auntie May replied. "Because he *did* have an affair—"

"Same deal with Ms. Mui, right?" I interrupted.

"—with Mrs. Chan."

A brocha. This just kept getting richer.

"Lung Wong, pretending to be Ken Chan, was having an affair with Mrs. Chan," I said.

"He lived in their home; it was inevitable. She was the love of his life. The deep, abiding, one and true love. Maggie is twenty-five years younger than Sifu Chan. Is it any wonder, even loving him, that being separated she might succumb?"

"No," I admitted. I'd done foolish things too, and then done them again. More important, such love could account for his wishful look at the ring, longing for what he could never truly have. It would also explain what I had noted at the time, the unusually astringent faces of the family at the wake. Why May wasn't happy when Maggie took me aside. And why Lung's remains were hustled away so quickly. He had shamed the school . . . or at least the *sifu*. The afternoon must have been utterly unendurable for Mrs. Chan.

I was watching Auntie May. Her lips were moving again, very slightly, as they had at the deli. It was as if she were getting ready to say, *'But wait! There's more!'* And sure enough, there was.

"The situation was dire enough," she said. "But what made it worse was the fact that Lung was also seeing Chingmy Mui. It is, in fact, his child she is carrying. He had admitted that from the start."

"Proven by DNA testing?"

"There was no need," Auntie May said. "Chingmy was a virgin."

"So says who?"

"Her OB/GYN," Auntie May said.

"What, you just went in and asked?"

"I went in for an appointment and someone looked at her file."

"Did Maggie know he was two-timing her?"

"You mean being unfaithful?"

"Yes."

"When he learned Chingmy was coming to the belt test and his face glowed," May said, "then Maggie knew. Women know when a man is no longer theirs."

"The Chinese are wiser than I am," I replied. "Did the Muis know that Lung was not Sifu Chan?"

"No," Auntie May replied. "One of the judges at the competition had to be informed, since he knew Sifu Chan from years before. He understood why. But to everyone else, Lung was Ken Chan."

"With all this *Prince and the Pauper* stuff going on, how did you propose to reintegrate the *sifu* when his work was finished?"

"We would have rejoined him in New York," she said. "There would have been no questions."

"So, to get back to the reason I'm here, the shooting," I said. "If the gunfire were directed at Lung Wong, it *could* have come from someone defending the honor of the cuckolded Sifu Chan."

"It is doubtful," Auntie May said. "That was a closely held secret."

"All right, then. From someone defending the honor of Chingmy Mui. Or someone from the gang in New York who believed he was the *sifu* and wanted him dead. Or someone from the gang in New York who somehow knew he was *not* the *sifu* and wanted to send a message to the real *sifu* that his school and possibly his family here were going to be attacked. There are a half dozen or more good reasons to have shot him, and probably a half dozen more bad ones I don't know about. Maybe it was the Li family seeking additional payback."

"Yes," Auntie May replied. "All of those are reasonable."

Her ledger-like mind served her well; I had already forgotten most of the things I had said.

"It's quite a tale," I replied thoughtfully, "but there is still one big problem with it. It doesn't explain the second and third attacks."

"Sadly, it does," she said. "A transfer from another school and our first black belt, Yuen Hung, was out riding his bike not far from where you were sitting the other night," May said. "He was heading in your direction, racing to get out of the rain, when the gunshots erupted. Yuen hid behind a tree and waited until the police arrived."

That would explain the clattering I heard and had forgotten about. Also, "heading in your direction" would mean he might not have been close enough to be picked up by Banko's vibrating doohickey wires. And given Yuen's location behind me, it was possible someone was trying to shoot him.

"And tonight?" I asked.

"Tonight, Mrs. Chan was trying to contact you."

"Then that was her on the phone?"

Auntie May nodded. "I warned her it was dangerous, but she felt that you needed to know the truth. This truth."

"Why did she call from a public telephone?"

"She is afraid to use her cell phone in case someone might use it to track her," Auntie May told me.

I was about to ask if gangs had that kind of triangulation technology, but that was stupid. Chinese hackers had been inside more American computers than Microsoft software.

I was mentally exhausted. And troubled by one thing more: while all of this fit, it did not necessarily bring us any closer to the identity of the shooter. Every Chinese-American on the dance card being pissed off at every other local Chinese-American did not necessarily mean they were trying to *kill* everyone else.

"How much of this have you shared with the police and the FBI?" I asked.

"They know that Lung Wong is not Ken Chan," she told me. "Agent Bowe-Pitt was entrusted with that knowledge after the killing. The NPD knows as well. Sifu Chan is working with the police in New York to uncover the gangs. They were in communication when Maggie informed them of this danger."

"Do you know if the NPD suspects that those New York gangs may have migrated south?"

"It must be the concern of someone or we would not have police protection at the school and at our apartments on Elmington Avenue," she said.

That was true. I wondered if she knew I had been kidnapped and grilled about Ken Chan. I decided not to tell her. If she knew anything, she would have mentioned it. If she had been involved, she wouldn't exactly be forthcoming. So—no point.

"Where is Mrs. Chan now?" I asked.

"At home," she said. "She is safe. Students are also watching the residence."

"Right. I'm assuming they don't know that she was having an affair with a man who wasn't really her husband . . . because they thought he *was* her husband."

Auntie May nodded once. "He went home with them. He slept there. What reason had they to think otherwise?"

I sat there like a cold blintz as I let all of this seep into my tired brain. Then something occurred to me.

"Auntie May, with all that has happened over the past few days—do you know where the real Sifu Chan has been? Has anyone spoken to him?"

For the first time since I met her, a question made the woman squirm. "We have not spoken with him," she replied. "We do not know where he is. Neither do the police. He has disappeared."

"Disappeared as in he stopped calling people? Or disappeared as in . . ." I let the silence finish the thought.

"Detective Daniels has been looking into that with the NYPD," she said. "They have one clue."

"Which is?"

She seemed close to tears. She shut her eyes. The woman's tiny hands were resting on her lap.

I rested one of mine on top, intending to give her comfort—and squealed with pain as she gripped my fingers with the chicken-claw digits of her left hand and twisted my hand so my palm was facing upward, my knuckles resting on her sharp knee and my fingers tortured backward over the side, toward the floor. My hand was pinned there, and my shoulder slumped toward her fast to relieve the awful, stabbing pain that poured up each finger into my wrist, where it exploded into something worse.

The entire thing took no more than a second. One second. Auntie May opened her eyes, gasped, released me, and sat back in her chair, recoiling from me as though I were a scorpion in a cigar box.

I grabbed my poor hand with the other and lifted it; my wrist was that weak and useless from what she'd done.

"I am so sorry," she said. "So sorry."

"Wow! That *hurt!*"

"Please forgive me. It—it was a reflex."

"I noticed! So you know martial arts too! I didn't realize—"

"Yes, our entire family was schooled in the Shaolin arts—I am so deeply sorry."

Sensation other than anguish was beginning to return to a forearm, which felt, for lack of a better comparison at that pained moment, like a floppy rubber dildo. I shook it lightly to restore some calm to the jangled nerves. When I was

done, I laid it back on my own knee, palm down.
It still pained me around the wrist.

"You were about to say something about the
one clue to Sifu Chan's disappearance?" I said,
wincing.

She regained her composure. "Telephone
records show that he received a call from Nashville."

"Do you know from whom?" I asked.

"We do not," she replied. "We only know that
it came from the main number at the Nashville
Police Station."

Chapter 17

When I reached the deli after a long "walk" with my cats, it occurred to me that I should send all the cops home and just have Auntie May stay at the deli. That *tante* was a badass. My wrist still hurt when I moved it.

But it didn't hurt as much as my brain. It was like something out of Alexandre Dumas, but in English and Chinese.

Ken Chan, the real one, was working in New York, undercover, helping the NYPD bust the gang, or gangs, that had been sending soldiers to train at his school. Who, besides Chan's close family, Auntie May, and the late Lung Wong—who was a student, also from New York—knew that?

Ken Chan, the real one, also hadn't been heard from by anyone since the day of the first shooting. On that day, someone from the NPD called his cell phone. Presumably, no one at the NPD knew that Ken Chan was still in New York.

However, that one wasn't too difficult to explain: the NPD had recovered a cell phone at the deli that was likely registered to Lung Wong, not Ken Chan.

Lung Wong, the fake Ken Chan, had been in Nashville for six months with the rest of the real Chan clan. They were not quite hiding, but they were presumably off the radar of the New York gangs.

Lung Wong had briefly dated Chingmy Mui and gotten her pregnant. Lung Wong was also having an affair with Ken Chan's wife, Maggie.

Somewhere in all that were at least two people who had abducted me. Two people who wanted to know about Lung Wong's final moments, thinking they were Ken Chan's final moments or thinking that *I* thought they were Ken Chan's final moments. The kidnappers could have been from the Mui family, scouts of the New York gangs, or peeved members of the Chan clan. It was possible, I told myself, that the gangs had either killed the real Ken Chan—which is why he was silent—or had learned he was after them and wanted family members as hostages. If so, I hoped they tried to take Auntie May first. They'd never see her little wrist-twist action coming.

Then there was the gunman . . . or gunmen. They could be Chinese trying to kill Chinese. Maybe the gunmen were New York gang *shmeckles*. Or they could be SSS guys who didn't like Jews *or* the new Chinese in town. Maybe the arrival of the kung fu family had pushed them over the edge. Maybe they were shooting at all of us.

And don't rule out Banko Juarez, I reminded myself. Maybe he was an opportunist and had hired the second and third shooters. He could have been parked nearby tonight to get etheric readings of terror from me. Perhaps that's why he wasn't in his room when I called.

Plus there was always the stuff one didn't know, suspect, or imagine. Before tonight, that would have been pretty much everything I'd heard.

Could I even trust that? How did I know Auntie May wasn't making all this up for some reason only she knew?

I thought of running this all past Grant. If nothing else, I did trust the man. But I didn't want his overprotectiveness getting in the way of his, or my, investigation. Besides, I had a better idea. Or a worse one, depending on one's criteria.

I slept well in my makeshift bed on the floor, with the blended smells of Lysol, canola oil from the nearby deep fryer, and burned toast in my nose. The latter was from the toaster, which was nearby. My last conscious thought had been, *I gotta clean out the crumb catcher.*

My first conscious thought in the morning had nothing to do with food. It was to wonder who had called me at three AM. My cell phone was in the office, and though I heard the ring tone, I ignored it and fell back asleep. It was

Banko asking if I'd butt-dialed since I hadn't left a message. I'd call him later when I figured out exactly what I wanted to say.

The staff was horrified to see the new damage and to learn that I'd been shot at again. Thom immediately prayed. Of all the adjustments I'd made since coming down here, that was the one I was surprised to find went down easiest. I had always been a cynic about organized religion and dogma—as opposed to tradition. I loved a good *sukkah* construction project or *dreidel* spin or wedding *hora* as much as the next Jew. But ritual and showing up at a building so God can listen seemed a little controlling. Maybe it was, but I'd seen a charming correlation between folks Thom hung out with and generosity of spirit— as opposed to the me-ism of people who also seemed, not by coincidence, to have abandoned their faiths. I was coming to understand that the sense of community, in a church or in a martial arts school or even among my staff, was a corner- stone of civilized society.

When Thom prayed, I knew that, if she asked, her fellow churchgoers would pray—and care while they were doing it, because she cared. They wouldn't just phone it in. Maybe that also tied in with the stuff Banko went on about: energy. I didn't know enough to dismiss it, which is what I'd done when I knew even less.

Other than the guardians who stood front and back, the day was surprisingly lean on visits from law enforcement. The only reason I knew that the NPD was checking national gun registries to try to find the owner of the rifle was because I read it on a local news website. The difficulty was that there was no guarantee the weapon was local. Even if it were, that check alone would take a week or more.

We had another day of brisk business, though it was less than the day before. I had time to work with the insurance company adjuster and the glazier, who were going to work together to repair my window. I also asked the adjuster to kick in some money to repair the bullet holes in the floor. There was a box of extra tiles in the cellar. He said he'd take care of it and told me I'd have a check within a week. For all its joys and wonders, New York City would never have gotten this job done so quickly.

All in all, it was actually a pretty normal day until, like a world in which vampires or zombies rule, the sun went down, and then suddenly it wasn't so normal.

I received another call from the same pay phone. It was the same voice as the day before.

"Ms. Katz?"

"Yes."

"This is Maggie Chan," the caller said. "I must speak with you."

"All right."

"Not on the phone—I want to meet with you."

"I already got my insurance quote for bullet holes," I said. "What sheltered place and when?"

"How about the parking garage down the

street from you?" she said. "I saw your car at the school—I will know it again."

"When did you see it?" I asked.

"Last night."

"But you weren't at the school, were you?"

"No," she said. "I was in the police car."

"Why?"

"I was making arrangements for them to watch my daughter while I came to see you—again."

Another curve ball. If Maggie was tight with the NPD for some reason, that could explain the call to her husband's cell phone.

"All right," I said. "Let's do this."

I agreed to meet her in a half hour. I was being reckless and insane, I know. But the *megillah* Auntie May had spun, while fascinating, failed to clear up anything as it pertained to me. Maybe Maggie could add to my intel. She seemed keen to, for reasons that would no doubt benefit her as well.

I finished up my work with the late-afternoon crowd, left cleanup to the staff, and walked over to the garage. There were plenty of pedestrians still out, and I kept my eyes on the rooftops and windows across the street. Unless Maggie were plugged into the gunmen, I didn't see how they could know where I was going and when.

Of course, she *could* be plugged into the gunmen. Right now, nothing would surprise me.

I went down the ramp and saw Maggie waiting at my car. I greeted her and opened the passenger's side door. I got behind the wheel. We sat. She smelled faintly of the roses at the school. She was not the grieving ice queen I'd seen at the wake. She was dressed in jeans, a white blouse, and a New York Rangers baseball cap with the brim pulled low.

Go, Rangers. The girl was definitely from New York.

"I'm sorry you are involved in all of this," she said without preamble. "May I ask—what did Auntie May tell you?"

"You have an hour?" I asked.

"Yes."

Oh. It was going to be one of those kinds of meetings, I thought. "Sorry, that was a joke," I said, and proceeded to recount everything the older woman had said. Maggie listened without comment. When I was finished, I asked, "So how much of that is true?"

Maggie tipped the brim back and looked at me with big, sad eyes, "All of it, except for one thing: I was not having an affair with Lung Wong."

And there was another sharp turn in a tale already full of right angles. "Why would Auntie May make that up?" I asked, dubious and annoyed. I am never happy when I am being played.

"She wanted you to think that Lung Wong was more committed to me than he was to Chingmy."

"Why the heck would that matter?"

"Money," Maggie said.

That smelled like the truth. The two prime movers were now present in one neat little bundle: love and assets. "Go on," I told her.

"In the hierarchy of mistresses, the one who is truly beloved is valued higher than the one who is not. That goes back to the ancient dynasties. We have a saying: 'She who is loved most is not just treasured more but is worth more treasure'—even if the second or third woman is with child. The fault for having misjudged a man and conceived an offspring falls upon the shoulders of a woman."

"I'm confused," I said. "Not the part about the misogyny, that nonsense I understand, unfortunately—it's always the lady's fault. What I don't get is why Lung didn't just tell the Muis the truth about his situation?"

"Which truth?"

"He could have told them that he isn't Ken Chan and wasn't married to you," I said. "He could have married Chingmy in secret or simply waited until your husband came back, free of his obligations in New York."

"Lung could not do that because he already *has* a family in New York," Maggie informed me.

Oh, come on, I thought. This was like a plate piled high with *lokshen,* Jewish spaghetti.

"It's true," Maggie went on, responding to my obvious disbelief. "Lung fathered a child with the sister of one of the gang leaders and married her. They expected him to join the family business."

"The triads?" I asked.

"Yes. You've heard of them?"

I was about to say, "*Lung told me . . .*" but stopped myself. Chinese folks were too keen to know what the dead man said to me at our brief meeting. The fewer people who knew, the safer I might be. Instead I just nodded.

"Lung was sweet, and a skilled fighter, and very giving—as you well know. But he was also very, very naive. He loved quickly, he loved thoroughly, and it blinded him to everything else, just as it did with Chingmy Mui. Instead of joining the gangsters, he went into hiding at a massage parlor his Aunt May owned."

"A massage parlor?"

"For the feet and back," she said. "It was legitimate. Auntie May secretly owns several, all very lucrative."

That little closet Jew, I thought. The *Chasids,* the Orthodox, own most of the escort services in Manhattan.

"The situation with Lung is why my husband stayed behind," Maggie went on. "The gang leader threatened to kill him, May, and anyone else affiliated with the school unless Lung fulfilled his obligations."

"To become a father and a gangster? No exceptions."

"That is their way," Maggie said. "And our way

is that the responsibilities of one become the responsibility of all. My husband had no choice but to defend him."

"By working with the NYPD."

"Yes."

"So, as I told Auntie May, if Lung was looking at the ring on his finger when he was shot— you're saying that he was *not* thinking of you, as Auntie May said. He was thinking of his real wife back in New York—or possibly of Chingmy, whom he couldn't have."

"That is correct. We will never know who, though he was infatuated with Chingmy."

"And damned virile," I said. "Two women, two kids. But I still don't get why Auntie May would lie to *me*—though it does explain why she gave you a puss when you took me in the office."

"Gave me—?"

"A puss. Made a face."

"Yes. She said she believes the Muis kidnapped you and might do so again. She was hoping that if this does occur you will reinforce the notion that Lung loved me more than Chingmy."

"How does that help? The fact is, there would still be two women in his life: either you and Chingmy or the triad wife and Chingmy."

"The Muis didn't know about the triad wife. They *couldn't* know or they would have to know the truth about Lung. Then they could have threatened to tell the gangsters where to find him unless May paid up. In fairness, they are only looking to the future of Chingmy and the honorable size of her dowry."

"So Auntie May needed another lover for her nephew—you—or the Muis would have full access to her wealth."

"Yes. And she would be honor-bound to pay it. This way, the Muis will end up with a much, much smaller percentage. Especially because he was living with me, not Chingmy."

"Possession is nine-tenths of the law," I said. "And I'm guessing that even with Lung dead, the responsibility remains in place."

"Very much so," Maggie said. "If Lung was committed to Chingmy above all, the Wong family would still be expected to provide for the child for the rest of its life and Chingmy until she remarried. Your alimony laws owe a great deal to the Chinese. Though it is not like America in this sense: with us, grandparents, aunts and uncles, and even first cousins are often held responsible for the debts of a deadbeat father."

"That actually sounds kind of fair," I said. "Why should the child suffer?"

"I agree in theory," she replied. "The problem is, Auntie May also owns the bulk of the stock in our school. If she is financially stressed, it impacts us all."

Woe betide the wayward son. And they say Jews are preoccupied with money and schemes. Auntie May had us beat. She was not only tight, she was the queen of the *ligners,* a liar whose fantastic narrative ranked with other classic *bubbe meises.*

"Let me ask you this, then," I said. "How would the Muis possibly have benefited by kidnapping me?"

"That's the main reason I wanted to see you," she said. "When Lung signed the receipt, did he sign in English or Chinese letters?"

"My abductor asked me that."

"Of course."

"Why 'of course'?"

"I'll get to that in a minute," Maggie told me. "What did you say?"

"I said I couldn't remember, and I don't. Most signatures are illegible, so I don't bother to look too closely. Anyway, the police have them now. I don't know when I'll get them back. Why does it matter?"

"Because the Muis threatened to forge letters of commitment to Chingmy if he did not honor his obligation," Maggie said.

"That doesn't seem honorable."

"Dishonor in the support of a greater honor is not deemed wrong," she said.

There was a curious logic to that, I had to admit.

"Lung Wong never signed receipts at the school," Maggie said. "Auntie May did that. He did not sign certificates of promotion. We used a rubber stamp of my husband's signature, for obvious reasons. If the Muis were to obtain a sample of Lung's writing to forge such letters, they would accidentally have discovered that he was not Ken Chan."

"And if that became common knowledge, the gangsters might hear of it," I said.

"Yes. Do not forget: it is Lung Wong who disappeared, not Ken Chan. As far as the world is concerned, Ken Chan moved to Nashville."

"You really think the Muis would risk a kidnapping charge and a couple of decades in prison just to get Lung's autograph?"

"In matters of face, especially that of a daughter who is an unwed mother, there *is* no other consideration."

That made sense, I guess. Their Asian brethren in Japan cut their bellies open as a point of honor.

"Back at the school you asked me about the wedding ring," I said. "Why did that matter to you?"

"Wearing it, treasuring it, displaying it would have been an uncharacteristic but tangible expression that his wife—me—was number one, not his mistress."

"So Lung was aware this problem was coming and looking to protect the family finances."

"Yes."

"I see," I said. Then something else occurred to me. "Hold on. Lung, posing as your husband, judged that competition in Atlanta.

Wouldn't the gangsters have noticed he wasn't Sifu Chan? "

"It was a risk we had to take," Maggie said. "When our students became finalists, there was no way for Lung to avoid serving as a judge. The region's top-ranked *sifus* are required to do so. Fortunately, the competition received very little coverage outside the Southeast and the martial arts community—"

"Those clippings on the wall of the office."

"That's right. And, again, the gangsters were searching for Lung, not my husband. They would not have paid attention to reports about Ken Chan at a regional competition. We made sure he did not appear in photographs, or that he appeared with his head in motion or turned away. It annoyed the picture-takers but protected us."

"Which makes me wonder, why *didn't* the triads come down here looking for Lung? If they know the school is here, wouldn't that be the logical place to look?"

"Yes, which is why my husband agreed to help the NYPD keep them very, very busy up north," she said. "Ken has been watching them carefully. He knows the people, the streets, how to hide in plain sight. He has been living in one of the massage parlors, coming out only at night. It has been hard on him."

"Yes. A man living in a massage parlor. Awful."

That hurt her, and I was sorry. I said so. My

tragic experiences with men have their own life and will, which I cannot always control.

"There have been arrests," she went on. "We speak once a day on a special telephone. He believes they are making real progress."

"But the triads are not yet broken."

"No. For the last six months they have been cautious, but that may have changed this past week."

"The shooting."

She nodded. "Perhaps someone finally identified my husband in Chinatown, realized he is not the one who claims to be Ken Chan down here. The triads may have sent someone to check. They may have driven past the school and recognized Lung. Worse for me and my daughter, they may be seeking further retribution—not just for Lung, but now for the arrests in Chinatown."

"Which is the reason for the police car. And maybe the gunfire last night."

She nodded again.

"You've got to be terribly worried—"

"Every minute of every day."

I was going to comfort her with a pat on the arm, but remembered what Auntie May had done to my hand. I refrained.

I drove Maggie back to the school, and we parted with smiles and silence. We both had a lot on our minds. I was trying to process all the new information and see which parts of it impacted me directly. Except that a bunch of people thought Lung Wong, alias Ken Chan, may have said something important to me, or that I might have Lung's John Hancock—which put me at risk of abduction or death—the details didn't seem to matter. Not that those weren't big things, mind you; it's just there was nothing I could do about any of it. That was the job of the FBI and the NPD.

I will say this much: my crash course in Chinese culture was fascinating. Their society and codes of conduct had more layers than a *kugel,* and it was as orderly as any of my uncle's recipes. Culturally, emotionally, and socially, Jews are all over the place. I wasn't used to a tradition of such severe logic and absolute results. I remember one of my uncles and another man, Shmuely, haggling over the price of a rack of dresses on Broadway and 26th Street; the argument escalated to the point that my uncle actually put together a group of investors to approach Shmuely's partner and buy his share, just to harass him. In retaliation, Shmuely sold his share to my uncle, went to Taiwan, started a rival dressmaking firm, and ended up putting my uncle out of business. Jewish life is fluid like that.

That said, the parry and riposte and counterthrusts of the Chinese were enough to make your head spin. I longed for my home, my bed, my couch . . . not the office and sleeping on the floor.

Of course, that's not where I ended up. Instead, I went where I needed to be for my own safety, back under the toaster whose crumb catcher I still had not cleaned.

Chapter 18

I was awakened by a commotion at the back door.

". . . not here."

"Officer, I know she is. At least, her phone is. I just called it."

It was Banko. I had been so out of it I hadn't heard the ring tone; my pal pulled the same trick I had without knowing I had pulled it.

I rolled my head to the side and looked at the clock over the kitchen door. It was three AM.

"Look, I just got back into town and I need to—"

"It's okay!" I shouted, rising from my rumpled bag like a wraith from the grave. "I'm coming!"

The uproar ceased, and I threw the bolt. The officer had her hand on her gun butt. Either Banko hadn't noticed or he was so obsessed he didn't care. My guess was both. The etherical pioneer looked tired and disheveled, as though—well, as though he'd just taken a long journey and had come here without showering or changing his clothes.

He came in uninvited, his laptop case thrown over his shoulder. I left the door open and mouthed a "thank you" at the officer. We went to the dining room, me following Banko.

"That kinship reading from the other morning has been bugging me," he said without a howdy-do. And, apparently, those semi-matching readings he got now had an official name. "You know why? Because it was fainter than the others. Not by much, but by enough to make it stand out. Or stand down, really."

"Meaning what?"

I was asking that a lot, I realized. Having Banko or Auntie May or Maggie or the hypnotist clarify things. Life was easier, if less entertaining, when the only thing anyone talked about was finance. I ran from it, but I wondered if maybe that predictability was a good thing for my need to control stuff.

Banko opened his laptop and booted it to illustrate. I wouldn't know what I was looking at, but it made him feel better. Of course, I still had the issue of pimping to discuss with him, but that could wait.

"Normally, the readings directly behind me are as strong as those in front or to the sides," he said. "Even though they have to go through sinew and organs, my tissues act as an amplifier. That would not be the case for someone who was moving quickly through the field."

"Like one of my waitstaff."

"Exactly, exactly. But look at this line." He brought up the mass of squiggles and isolated one, dimming the others. "It's about seventy percent as strong as the rest. That tells me someone was probably outside, out front."

"So? They could have been waiting for someone to pick them up."

"That's right! *Or* they could have been standing there as a target for someone to line up a rifle shot," he said.

I looked over at the plywood window, tried to imagine someone out there. "That's a big leap," I pointed out. "A mighty big leap."

"But not impossible."

"No."

"Good," he said. "So we have kinship readings at two shootings. There's more." He sounded like one of those TV salespeople who howls, "*But wait! If you order now . . .*" Standing hunched over his keyboard, bringing up data I still wasn't convinced had a scintilla of validity, he showed me a reading he had taken the day before the shooting of Lung Wong. It matched the one that was taken allegedly outside my deli. "Someone was a bad boy. And look," he said, pointing proudly. "A time stamp. We know when he was at the hotel."

I had been hunched beside him and straightened. If the readings *were* accurate, it meant that our mystery person, who was related to another mystery person at the park, had also paid for sex.

"If we can get the concierge at the hotel to tell us who was there at that time, we'll know who was outside your deli," Banko said proudly.

"How are we going to do that?" I asked. "Do you, y'know, happen to have any suction there?"

"Suction? Yes. I room there often."

"Nothing stronger than that?"

His lids lowered as he suddenly recalled our previous conversation. "That's the second time you've asked about my ties to that place. What's going on?"

"It's a fancy brothel."

"Not entirely, but so what? I told you why I stay there."

"For the readings," I said.

"For the readings. It's like Jane Goodall living with chimps. That doesn't make her a monkey."

It would if she were animal finding companions for Jungle Jim, my tired mind thought before I could stop it. I decided to give round two a rest. There were more important matters at hand than busting Banko Juarez.

"I'm sorry, I'm just tired," I told him, doing my best to pretend I was wrong, had crossed a line. "I'm not used to this. We move in different social circles."

"It's no great honor being ahead of the curve," Banko said immodestly and in earnest—a nauseating combination. I would've barfed, but I had neglected to have dinner.

"Lay on, Macduff," I said, grabbing my keys

and a bag of oyster crackers sitting on a shelf by the back door as we headed out. Both police officers, fore and aft, expressed concern about my leaving; I assured them I was in good hands. I wasn't sure of that, of course, and I kept an eye trained on the rooftops across the street as we emerged from the alley.

I was expecting to drive, but I found that Banko had a car sitting by the curb.

"I thought you took a train to Clarksville," I said.

He grinned. "That was a joke. I'm a big Monkees fan. I couldn't resist."

"So—you lied to me."

"Not lied," he said. "Had some fun is what I did."

A joke in the midst of murder, attempted murder, and kidnapping. I had to give the guy credit for being able to compartmentalize.

As we drove to the hotel, I realized that this was the first time since I'd been down here that I felt that events were more or less completely out of my control. In the other matters, bad things had happened to people I didn't know or people I barely knew. I could dip my toe in, get out, then go back in. Even when I had gotten tangled up with the wiccans, that had been a choice I made, albeit with unexpected results.

In this case, things were happening *to* me. And not just on one front but on two. For all

I knew, something else could happen at any moment.

"It really should be legal anyway," I said, as we neared the hotel. "Our bodies, ourselves."

"Huh?"

"Prostitution."

Banko scowled. "Do you ever think of anything else?"

"Not when I'm headed to a house of ill repute," I said. "Which isn't often, mind you. In fact, this is just the third time that I'm aware of."

"Do what I do, think of it as just a laboratory," he said. "You'll find the experience a lot more productive."

Once again, he seemed sincere. I had to wonder if Richard Richards had lied to me; but if so, why? After the way Auntie May and Maggie had knocked my brain around, and given the fact that it was ridiculously early in the morning, the soil was ripe for conspiracy theories. Was Richards, in fact, planting that evidence on Banko's computer? Was *he* a pimp or taking protection money from the hotel or a member of the frequent fornicators club? Hopefully, some answers lay down the street. And no, the pun wasn't intentional . . . but I'll take it.

There was a big doorman looking the other way as we hurried past. It was quiet at this time of night, with more people leaving quickly, behind scarves or high collars, than were mingling at the bar. We walked over to the desk. The night clerk recognized me and gave me a sly little grin.

"It's a little late for the sexual healer," she said with a wink. "Her hours are nine to six. Or are you going for another round with this New Age fruit?"

It took me a second to get her meaning. She was talking about the third member of the therapy trifecta.

"Neither," I replied. "Mr. Juarez and I are here to find someone who may be an accessory to homicide."

The woman's smirk vanished like steam from chicken soup. It set off tiny alarm bells in my newly sensitized brain.

"Banko, why don't you sit somewhere and do things on your computer," I said.

"What? Why?"

"Just go. Check your graphs or something. Make new ones. I just want a few moments alone with Bananas."

I hoped he got my meaning. He didn't seem to, making a disgusted sound as he walked to one of the love seats in the center of the lobby.

I turned back to the woman. "I need to know more about Banko Juarez, that man I was with," I said. "How well do you know him?"

"You law enforcement?" she asked.

"No. God, no. I don't even like dating cops."

That seemed to relax her a little. "He comes and goes, like most people here," she said. "Except for some of the ladies."

"He isn't . . . he doesn't manage any of them, does he?"

"Honey, I see him around. He pays his bills. I don't ask about his business arrangements."

"That's fair," I said.

"Why are you interested in homicide?" she asked. "Friend of yours get hurt?"

"In that deli shooting the other day," I said.

"The martial arts guy?"

I nodded.

"I heard about it. Sad, sad thing," she said.

I nodded again.

She nodded now, this time toward Banko. "You think he had something to do with it?"

"I don't know."

"What makes you think that?"

"He was there that morning, asking a lot of questions, casing the place out. The whole thing was very suspicious."

"I assume you told the cops?"

"Sure. They checked him out, couldn't find anything. Except that maybe he was involved with illegal operations." I shrugged. "Maybe someone was trying to send *him* a message. I don't know."

"Yeah. So why are you hanging out with him?"

"You know what they say," I said.

"Keep your enemies close?"

"No," I replied. "*Az me ken nit ariber, gait men arunter.*"

"Excuse me?"

"It means, *If you can't go over, go under,*" I told her. "It's Yiddish, the language of a group of European Jews."

Bananas smiled sweetly. "How cute that you know it. But I still don't get what you mean by what you just said."

"I was referring to the different ways of getting things done. Some people prefer taking a path of less resistance. Others are more aggressive. They prefer violence. Shock, shooting, slaughter, that kind of thing."

The smile folded in on itself.

We stared at each other for a moment longer, after which I left with a little smile and walked to the love seat where Banko was working on his computer. His hands were cupped alongside his little gadget. He was focused on the screen, which I couldn't see because of the angle.

"That was further than I intended to go," I said.

"Huh?"

"Nothing. I guess I was angrier than I thought. Or more tired. What've you got?"

"You're brilliant," he said, still without looking up.

That was something I liked to hear. I leaned in. The screen was split, top and bottom. On top were the three lines he was trying to match. Below it were new lines. "It scares me," I told him.

"What does?"

"That I know what I'm looking at."

I did, too. There were five people in the lobby:

Banko, me, a guest, a bartender, and our friend
Bananas. Three of the lines matched the three
lines on top.

"Are you sure there's no one making squiggly
lines from the outside, upstairs, anything like
that?" I asked.

"I'm sure."

Just then, the guest left and his line winked
out. That left four lines and three matches. The
bartender moved away. One line got a little
smaller. Clearly, it wasn't his line that Banko had
recorded the other day.

"So I was right," I said, with a little bit of ice
running up my backbone. "Bananas was outside
the deli."

"There's no other explanation," Banko said.

Well, there was. The software could be flawed,
Banko could be nuts, or both. But my exchange
with Bananas confirmed that she was a least a
little bit hostile. Maybe not enough to be an accessory to murder, but worrisome enough.

I considered that as I looked back at her.
Bananas was staring at us. And not with her
normally bemused look but with something
pointy and dangerous. She did not turn away
when I caught her staring. Our eyes remained
locked. That gave me an even bigger chill.
She picked up the phone. My spine was now
below freezing.

"I think it's time for me to go," I said, "and can
I make a suggestion?"

"Sure."

"You probably shouldn't stay here tonight," I said.

"Why?" He regarded me with what seemed to be a genuinely confused little boy look, like I'd told him he couldn't go outside and play.

"Because I think Bananas is getting ready to live up to her namesake."

Banko shut his computer after saving the data. As we rose, a door to the left of the front desk opened, and two men came out. They were big, beefy white men—security types. We started toward the door, quickly.

Unfortunately, we did not make it outside.

Chapter 19

Our way was blocked by the big doorman. He looked like a big, bad biker. His long, black hair was pulled back in a ponytail. He wore a full beard knotted at the bottom and had on sunglasses that didn't quite cover the big mole under his right eye. A snake tattoo went from one hand to the other.

"Give me your wristwatch," he said to me. "Quickly."

I thought I recognized the voice, but I was too stunned and too frightened to think about it—or to argue. I handed over the old Bulova from Korvette's, and he crushed it in his meaty hand. It was a bat mitzvah gift from my father. This was not the time to look for symbols and metaphors in what had just happened.

"Run in opposite directions," the doorman ordered. "*Now.*"

The surprise of *that* statement lasted about a

second as I placed the voice and looked up at the face again.

"Agent Bowe-Pitt?" I whispered. It wasn't actually a whisper; it was more like a frightened croak, which was the best I could manage.

"*Run! Leave the car and go back to the deli,*" he hissed, looking past us, into the lobby. "I'll see you tomorrow morning."

Technically it *was* the morning, but I didn't stand there and argue. I went to the right, and off my push, Banko ran left. Bowe-Pitt made a half-hearted reach for me, out of sight of the lobby, but I managed to slip away while wondering what the hell had brought him here.

He said the SSS was getting fed cash from somewhere, I remembered. *Maybe he was checking this place out.*

Banko and I met back at the deli, where I made coffee and we sat in the dining area to catch our breath, and not just literally. That had been a scary exchange with Bananas, and I couldn't help but wonder if we'd set something in motion.

Not that it could be much worse than what's been happening, I thought.

"Do you think they're going to come after us?" Banko asked, as I set the full mugs on the table.

"I don't know," I said. "It depends on whether they're the ones who have been after me for the last few days."

"Who else could it be?"

"A bunch of crazy martial artists or gangsters," I said.

I told him about the Chinese. By the time I finished he was suitably depressed.

"I didn't realize that associating with you would require survival training," he said.

"But it comes with free coffee," I pointed out.

He didn't even smile. "All I wanted to do was study the planes of human existence. I never expected the Spanish Inquisition."

"So that's really and truly all you do," I said. "Read etheric lines."

"Yes. That's all. I'm not a pimp or a snake oil salesman. I don't even understand how that idea got into your head. If I weren't so scared I would really resent it."

It got there because Richard Richards put it there, I thought. *Why would he do that if it weren't true? Could it have anything to do with what had happened tonight? Was he getting a kickback for cleaning up their records on police computers? How would harming Banko help that?*

"Why indeed?" I asked, staring into my own reflection in the cup. I still didn't want to bring up specifics to Banko. I didn't want him freaking out.

"Why what?" he asked.

"Why would someone lie about someone else?"

"Jeez, that isn't too broad a question."

"People lie about other people to gain something," I persisted. "Can you think of another reason?"

"Revenge."

"That's still a gain," I said. "So my question is, what would someone gain by lying about you being a pimp?"

His shoulders collapsed. "Christ. That. Again."

"Yes, that again."

"Hey, shouldn't I be the one questioning your affiliations?"

"What do you mean?"

"You seemed to know the doorman back there. Or he knew you. How?"

"He's a fed," I said.

"Right. And I'm James Bond."

"He works for the FBI down here," I insisted. "He's been investigating hate crimes."

"At the hotel?"

"No—but it's a longer story than I care to go into. Though I have to say, he's a helluva makeup man."

"Is he the guy who spread lies about me?" Banko asked. "Maybe he saw me there, jumped to those nutty conclusions."

"It wasn't him."

"But *someone* said crap about me," Banko went on. "Who? A customer? Someone from another restaurant? A different cop?"

"C'mon, I'm not at liberty to say. Anyway, you *do* understand that I'm giving you the benefit of the doubt here. The question is not who but why would someone lie?"

"I don't know, and this is just stupid. You're tired or you'd see that."

"Yes, I'm tired, but let's try it. Throw away that low self-esteem—"

"What?"

"Banko, you're in a crazy business. People knock you, so you keep to yourself. Even the hotel concierge called you a New Age fruit."

"That hussy called *me* names?"

"Exactly. Why would someone do just the opposite? Why would someone be afraid enough to discredit you?"

"Because I'm right about human energy being like fingerprints," he said.

That was still a lot to accept. But then I tapped my cup thoughtfully, causing my reflection to ripple. It settled quickly back into my image. Even my face in java, a completely different medium, reverted to a form that was still identifiably me.

Pseudo-science or not, Richards apparently feared it, I thought. What did he think the etheric record did, could, or might possibly show? The only person who was doing anything remotely suspect was Bananas. Agent Bowe-Pitt's own investigation had brought him to that hotel independently. But if Richards couldn't read the energy lines, how would he know that Bananas was among them . . . unless he already *knew* she had been present and didn't want that to be revealed? Why would he even care? Unless—

"No," I said.

"What?"

"It could be that the person who lied about you is involved," I said. "That's the only explanation that makes sense."

And that opened a slew of other questions. The NPD was aware of Ken Chan's activities in New York. The NPD was aware of the SSS activities in Nashville. Which of those was Richards and the hotel involved with?

There was one way to find out. I had to get back on the horse that didn't seem to want me enough to throw me.

I gave Banko the air mattress and napped in my office chair until I heard Thom scream. She had discovered my guest when she switched on the lights in the now-dark dining room. Happily, the day got no more exciting than that. Banko decided to head to a local computer café to answer e-mails. Wisely, other than to recover his car, he had no intention of going back to the hotel.

I waited until about ten before I put in a call that had my heart fibrillating just a tad. For the first time in a long time, I was calling someone for a date. What made it worse was that the someone hadn't shown any interest in me.

Richard Richards answered on the back end of a slurp.

"This is Richards."

"Hi—it's Gwen Katz. Of Murray's Deli."

"How are you?" he said without too much enthusiasm—but enough to make me not hang up.

"For a human target, I'm not bad," I said.

"Yes, I heard about those other incidents," he said. "It's awful what's going on. But you still have police protection at your place of business?"

"Yes, thanks. Hey, I was wondering—totally unrelated to anything about me being shot at—would you like to have a drink later?" The question hung there again, like last time, so I added quickly, "I have some questions about the work you were doing. That was pretty fascinating stuff."

"Computer forensics?" he said.

"Yeah. I used to wonder how some of my old Wall Street buddies cooked their computer logs," I lied.

My feigned interest made me ashamed . . . and a little worried. Granted, lack of sleep was partly responsible for my skewed reactions. But if my simple wiles failed—

They didn't.

"Sure, I'll be happy to talk about data fraud," he said, with a hint more enthusiasm. "Only thing is, I teach a class tonight."

"Really? I didn't know that was something you did." Ordinarily, I would have made a joke, like, "Community service?" To my credit, I refrained.

"Yes, I lecture once a week on cybersecurity," he said.

"Hey, that sounds like it could answer some of the things I wanted to ask. Would it be a terrible inconvenience if I tagged along?"

"I don't see why it should be," he said—a drop

in the enthusiasm scale. "Why don't I swing by there at seven?"

Score! Thank God something broke my way. "Perfect," I said. "I'll pack snacks if you'd like."

"That won't be necessary, but I appreciate the thought," he said politely.

"You're *sure* this isn't an imposition," I said.

"Not at all," he replied.

"Okay. Great. Terrific. See you tonight."

"Bye."

The "bye" was flat, unexcited. I hung up feeling unkosher. Not *glatt.* I've gotten more enthusiasm from gay men, and I didn't think Richards was gay. He had seemed nice enough when we met, if a little shy when I pitched my woo; this time he was a little standoffish. Or maybe he's just distracted?

Isn't that how you are when you're working? I asked myself. *Maybe you caught him in the middle of something and he was too polite to say so. Or maybe he heard about me and Grant and doesn't want any part of that.*

That actually made some sense, and it calmed my stretched nerves and bruised ego. I reminded myself that, in any case, this wasn't about me. It was about trying to find out why Richard Richards lied about Banko.

The highlight of the morning was the arrival of the glaziers with my new window. I was accustomed to seeing the shadow of the painted words "Murray's Deli" cast over the diner, but *gloib mir,* it was great having light back in my life. We were still doing takeout only. The staff and the few customers in line outside actually applauded when the big picture window was in place. The sign painter came that afternoon. I know that both veteran tradesmen had put me at the front of the line, a tribute to the high regard they had for my uncle. I also got the sense it was their way of speaking for the rest of Nashville: *Don't go. Whatever is behind this, we're behind you.*

That afternoon, around three, I got a visit from Bowe-Pitt, minus the motorcycle club accoutrements. He asked to see me in my office. Well, I was in the office anyway. Once again he was in the corridor. His big self absorbed the sound of our conversation.

"You know, it's a very bad idea to go nosing around the edges of this thing," he said. He was uncharacteristically stern, visibly annoyed. His moon face had angry little creases around the eyes.

"I do know that," I replied.

"You almost compromised my operation last night," he said.

"Sorry. Were you able to—"

"I said I grabbed your wrist, but this came off." He handed me my watch. The leather strap was torn, the buckle crushed. "I think they believed me."

"Again, I apologize. Did you learn anything?"

"That is not your concern," he said. "Your

job is to stay alive until the NPD and I have apprehended whoever is behind the shootings."

I couldn't dispute that and didn't. "Just tell me this," I said. "Do you have any idea whether my abduction and the shootings are connected?"

"There is one connection—you. That is why you have to stay here, under police protection, until we break this. Am I clear?"

I have a problem with someone telling me what to do, especially if that someone is a man. Even if he means well and especially when he runs the playbook that assumes that I'm a helpless female. So I looked up at the big boy and said, "You're clear. You want me to stay in my cage—"

"We call it an ISH—an Improvised Safe House."

"I call it Ish Kabibble," I said. "The bad guys know exactly where I am. My routine is predictable. I don't like that. I've got a new window, which means moving around in the dark and worrying that the enemy has night-vision goggles. I'd rather be a moving target than a stationary one."

"Detective Daniels has an officer on the roof across the street," he said. "I repeat: you are safe in here."

"Safe," I said. I realized then that I'd loaded a whole lot of bitterness on that one word. I had come down here to hide from the things I hated up north. I was already in a cage, and I didn't feel safe from aggressive men or corrupt attorneys or crooked fill-in-the-blank.

My *famisched* brain was a cage. I sighed. "Thanks for the visit, Agent Bowe-Pitt. Is there anything else you wanted to tell me?"

"Not in my professional capacity," he said.

Ouch. I couldn't tell if that was anti-Semitic, misogynistic, or just plain Gwen's-a-pain-in-the-*tuchas* but I'm not allowed to say that. I didn't care. He left and I sat there, determined to disregard everything he had told me. I hoped this was just a matter of flexing my shoulders and not a secret death wish. My exhausted mind and deflated spirits just weren't sure any more. Thinking back over the last five or so years, I wasn't even sure how I'd *gotten* to this point. Was it survival or hostility, a desire to be free or a hunger for change or both? Was it a natural evolution or a desperate fear of being in a rut, owned by a man or profession? Had I come here to shake up routine and push back against mortality—or to cut the waiting time by courting mortality?

Your subconscious is not your friend, Gwen bubbeleh, *and you need more sleep.* In a bed, not on the floor or in a chair.

The admitted fuzziness of my brain did make me question the wisdom of leaving here with Richards—but I told myself that whatever risk might be involved, I needed to know whether Banko Juarez and Richards and the NPD were my friend. That was something Bowe-Pitt did not seem in a position to tell me.

I kicked the office door shut with my toe. I

could feel the concern of my employees washing up against it. I didn't know what to say to them because I didn't know anything. That only strengthened my resolve to find out.

Though Bowe-Pitt was right about one thing. I should not leave here without a backup plan. All I had to do was figure out what one looked like . . .

Chapter 20

I had a bad feeling that my evening plans were going to go awry when Grant Daniels showed up at six forty-five.

We had closed the door at six in order to prep for a return to table service the following morning. Dani was busy cleaning up loose putty around the window. She was listening to her iPod and singing in her sweet soprano voice, so she was pretty oblivious. Not so the rest of my staff:

Thom was watching me like a *soykher* watching his cash register. Ironically, Thom's eyes should have been on the cash, not on me. I was going about my business, polishing the aluminum siding on the counter, feeling her gaze hot on my neck. I ignored her. My mind was elsewhere when I started shining the napkin holders that Dani had set on the table. I was standing over a table in the middle of the dining room, buffing the side of one holder with my shimmy, when I saw my warped reflection. I snapped back hard to the death of Lung Wong, and my knees wobbled.

"I knew it!" Thom said, rushing over. "I knew that was gonna happen!"

Luke and Newt ran from the kitchen. The two men hung back while Thom came to my side. She had her big, strong hand on my elbow, supporting me.

"I'm fine," I insisted. "Really."

"You're *not* fine! Remember that chocolate soufflé we tried to make for Lolo Baker's party? The one that caved in?"

"I am stronger than a cake, Thom."

"No you are not, woman! You nearly fell down just now."

"I wobbled like a Weeble, that's all—"

"That's baloney and you darn well know it! You are tired, and you are emotionally shot all to bread crumbs."

"Which is why I'm working, Thom," I said. "To keep my mind together."

"Honey, that has absolutely *not* been happening, and I've kept my mouth shut long enough."

I couldn't remember Thom ever failing to say exactly what was on her mind. "Have you?" I asked.

"About this, yes," she huffed. "You have been pouring it on for fourteen months without a break. And those haven't just been normal work months. They've been months filled with murder and other trials from the Lord God. You should be in your office finding a place to take a vacation."

"You know I don't do 'vacation.'"

"Well, you should. You most definitely should."

"Repeating everything won't make it true," I said defensively. "I would lose my mind sitting by a pool."

"You will lose your mind doing what you're doing!" she snapped back with a harsh tone and a side-to-side shift of her head that told me this girl means business. "Lawsy, I'm not the only one who feels this way. We all do."

I looked over at the cowering Luke and Newt. They looked small and frail, like acolytes in a temple when the gods went to war. Dani walked over to them from the kitchen and pulled her boyfriend away. Newt followed. Thom and I were alone in the dark diner. The sun was sinking fast, and we had not yet turned on the lights. Passing cars threw quick, sharp shadows against the floor and counter behind us.

"I know you mean well, Thom, and I appreciate it. Deeply. But that person you're describing, the one you want to be me, doesn't fit. And it isn't going to. For years, my former husband made me doubt everything I thought or felt or was. It got to the point where I believed his judgment more than my own. That was not only wrong; it was stupid. When I chucked that old life and came down here, I decided that, for better or worse, for richer or poorer, I was going to trust my instincts—"

"Even if they sent you down into the pit?"

I smiled inside. I could always count on Thom to bring in a religious metaphor. "My dear friend, I was *in* the pit. Up to my chin. I woke every morning with the smell of sulfur in my nostrils, my own screams of agony in my ears. Every time I've thought of giving up here, and there have been a few of those days, of handing you the keys and the business, I told myself, 'No. You're moving in the right direction.'"

"You're not just moving, you're there," she said. "That's the truth. Just by coming here you got free. You know what I see you doing? Digging a new-old pit."

"How?"

"By fighting everyone and everything that gets close to you," she said.

"You've got it backward, Thom. I just can't let anyone, anything, any emotion control me again."

And there, from my own mouth, I suddenly had clarity about Grant: it wasn't just his personality that didn't quite mesh with mine. It was how I felt trying to make myself fit with him that grated my skin raw.

Thom took my hands in hers. "You are strong and you are your own woman—we all know that. You have supported us when we were weak or breaking or broken. You don't need to keep proving how self-reliant you are, especially to yourself. Ezekiel saw the wheel way up in the air, and that wheel was run by faith. Why can't you have *faith*—not in God, though that would be nice, but in yourself, Gwen?"

I smiled, this time on the outside. "Thom—if I could do that, I'd be back on Wall Street making millions."

"You were too honest for that."

"No," I said. "I don't believe that Occupy crap. There were a few bad people, but most of us did right by our clients. But you had to go after those clients, make them yours. Risk their savings on a hunch and live with the occasional failure. It wasn't about honesty. It was about guts. I've been looking for mine here."

"So you risk yourself instead of your clients? Put yourself in harm's way?"

"I guess so," I said. "I would have been one of those nineteenth-century scientists who tried a new formula on herself before giving it to anyone else."

There were tears in Thom's eyes. She looked at me a moment longer, then hugged me tight.

"I wish you would believe," she said into my ear. "I have worked for a lot of people in my life, and I've never known anyone, not even your uncle, who had better instincts, who was a better employer, who gave better advice, and who related to workers and customers better than you. Lawsy, woman. Just *believe*."

That brought tears to my eyes, and as if on cue, the front door opened. Grant walked in, both sealing and ending the moment.

"Thanks," I said to Thom, as we parted.

"Everything okay?" Grant asked, seeing us together.

"Never better," I said.

"I saw the new window, just thought I would check in," he said, "make sure there wasn't any trouble."

It sure didn't sound as if Agent Bowe-Pitt had mentioned the previous night's adventure, and Richards apparently hadn't said a word about our little date.

"No trouble," I smiled.

He didn't know me well enough, or wasn't attuned enough, to know that I was lying. That was okay. To be fair, I hadn't really let him in that deep.

"Then sorry to interrupt," he said.

Grant looked around at the quietly busy staff, and then his eyes settled on me. I just stood there like Lot's wife. Another awkward moment in the multifaceted male-female saga of Gwen Katz.

"How are you?" I asked, just to ask something benign.

"Good." He started toward me. "By the way, there's nothing to report. Agent Bowe-Pitt is pursuing his own investigation while we're still working on the ballistics, rifle registry, surveillance video. Whoever is behind this has been very careful. We checked local chloroform sales, found nothing; that could have been bought out-of-state. Tough to track. Because the Feds are looking into the SSS, Detective Bean shifted from that mission and has been working with me on the Chinese connection."

"A thin black line," I murmured.

"What?"

"I was just thinking of the *sifu*'s black belt at the school. I'm guessing that even rivals close ranks against outsiders."

"Like you wouldn't believe," Grant laughed.

"Oh, I'd believe it," I said. "Jews are the same way."

"As are cops."

A Chrysler convertible pulled up out front. The roof was down. I saw the police sticker in the window, then I saw into the window. I swore inside my distracted head. Now that there was no longer a slab of plywood out front, Grant saw it too. He stared out at the street for a moment, then looked back at me.

"Uh-huh. Is this personal or professional?" he asked as he recognized Richard Richards in the driver's seat.

"If it were the former it would be none of your business," I said. That was a little harsh, so I added quickly, "I'm going to listen to his lecture on computer stuff."

Grant's mouth twisted. "Do you really think it's a good idea for you to go to the TSU campus?"

The question hit me like a big dollop of horseradish. I actually tasted the surprise in my mouth. I had not, in fact, realized that was where we were going. I figured it was at some community hall or high school or youth center.

"I'll be with a cop," I improvised. "No one will bother me, right?"

"If they do, you may not live long enough to know it!"

I pulled off my apron, grabbed my bag from the office, and headed toward the door. Grant hadn't moved. "I've got to go," I said to him, but included everyone with a final, sweeping look. "If you need me, call."

I stopped in the doorway. "I need to get out," I said to Grant.

"You've *been* out. That hasn't worked very well."

"I got attacked here, too. I've got to keep moving."

He came toward me. Everyone else, including me, was frozen.

"You're being stubborn and foolish," he said hotly.

"Wouldn't be the first time."

He stopped a foot away. "But it could be the last. Stay here until we bag and tag whatever is going on!" He looked over at my manager. "Tell her, Thom. Just be sensible for once."

We were both working on multiple levels here and Thom wisely held up both hands and walked away. Grant looked at me and lowered his voice. "Gwen, can't you see that I'm worried about you?"

"Yes. But muscling me isn't the way to help."

"That's not what I'm doing—"

"It is, Grant. You mean well, but I don't want to hide—especially since, when I hide, the bad guys know exactly where to find me. Three shots have been fired, two of them here. This is hardly a sanctuary." I glanced over at Richards, who had stayed in the car. I held up a finger to let him know I'd be right there. "Look, Grant— I've got to go."

I started out the door, and he grabbed my arm. I tensed but resisted pulling away.

I could tell from the way Grant's jaw grinded back and forth that he wanted to continue arguing. To his credit, he didn't. "Watch what's going on around you. Stay indoors as much as possible. And don't sit near any windows."

"All good ideas," I said. "Thanks."

I left then and hurried to the car, let myself in. Richards looked a little green. "Should we be doing this?" he asked.

"Why? Because of Grant?"

"Yeah, because of *Detective* Daniels. He's not my boss, but he is a superior—"

"He was afraid I was being reckless. I assured him I'm not. End of story."

He hesitated.

"Drive," I said encouragingly. "It's really okay." I flashed a big smile, one that was probably as inauthentic as oleo.

"If I don't I'll be late," he said. "Are you sure you want to come?"

In response, I buckled my seat belt. He gave a little shrug of resignation and pulled away, as I glanced back at the deli in my side mirror. Grant was standing in the door, looking sort of wounded and indignant, like Elijah just finding there was no cup for him at the Pesach table. I had a strong feeling he would definitely *not* be following me to the campus.

TSU. Whence I was fired at the other night. Grant, damn him, had a point: there *was* an element of recklessness to this if no one but Richards was there to back me up—and as far as I could tell in the glow of the instrument panel and the passing street lamps—he wasn't packing heat.

That was when I realized what my backup plan needed to be.

Chapter 21

The campus of Tennessee State University looked very different on a clear night than it did in a thick, misty rain. For one thing, there were students walking about, which put me somewhat at ease. On the other hand, there was nothing between me and the rooftops but open sky.

Not that I expected anyone to have parked in a crow's nest or rolled out a blood-red carpet for me. Unless Richards had given someone a heads-up, no one had known I was coming. Unless someone was following me, no one knew I was here.

Unless and unless, I thought. Far too many of those unlikely "what ifs . . . ?" had come along to bite me in the *tuchas* since I'd been down here.

Richards turned into a parking lot near the intersection of John A. Merritt Boulevard and 33rd Avenue N. The big William J. Hale Stadium loomed ahead.

"This is an arena gig then, eh?" I said.

"Clay Hall," he replied.

Those nine words doubled the number of words we had spoken during the short drive. Richards was not being rude, he was just being silent. I let him be, figuring he was reviewing the lesson plan in his head or thinking about work or wondering if Grant was going to ream him out in the morning.

He gave me a sideward glance; he didn't seem to get the joke.

"I have to stop at the administration building to get a key," he said, jerking a thumb to his left. "Would you mind waiting here?"

"No problem," I told him.

He left, and I sat, and the parking lot, though not quite empty, seemed unusually desolate now. I popped the door and leaned against the side of the car, then walked to and fro, then ranged a little farther.

Nervous much? I asked myself.

I looked at the few figures coming and going, at the students across the main road. I had the sudden urge to run forward, like the Ancient Mariner, and warn all the women about the future. Maybe I should teach a class: We're a Majority Being Treated as a Minority or How to Help Them Keep You Down. It occurred to me that so much of my overreaction—if that's what it was—to Grant and other men was cumulative. Not just what had happened to me, but what had happened to women around me. My mother, in

particular. So many Jewish families were matriarchies, yet that had to do with the home. In the
world, where I was, that accounted for *bubkes*.

I was beginning to feel chilly as a firm, cool
wind blew north, toward the main campus. I
looked back at the two-story, sandstone-colored
building. How the hell long did it take to get
a key?

Unless he was phoning for a sharpshooter, I
thought unpleasantly.

I got back in the car, sat, sent a text, checked
my phone for e-mails. I scrolled to my directory.
Looked at the names, wondered who I could
call. No one. No friends down here, dammit. I
got out of the car again, resolved to ditch the
night's plans and walk back to the deli—when
Richards reappeared, jogging from the building.
I felt relief, but it was relief that we'd be on the
move, not relief that I was safe, secure.

"Let's go," he said, scooting around the front
of the car and continuing on.

I guess we were walking to our destination. In
silence.

What the hell is wrong with this boy? I wondered
as I caught up. He was so talkative when we were
hacking Banko's computer.

We went to Clay Hall, which was in the direction opposite the stadium, on our side of the
main boulevard. It was in the belly of a slew
of buildings, any one of which could be a
sniper's roost.

But isn't, I told myself. *You're just going to a damn lecture.*

We entered the building; at least Richards held the door for me and allowed me to go first. Before he could enter, a young woman—one of his students, I assumed—ran up and started talking with him. I couldn't hear their discussion, but she was animated, his manner was brighter, and I felt worse than a third wheel: I was like *traif* on the menu, the uncleanest kind of shellfish. They entered the hallway slowly, chit-chattering away, and I suddenly did not want to be there anymore. I continued ahead, looking for an exit that would not force me to double back. Not that they would have noticed me.

There was a split corridor ahead, with an exit sign pointing left. I went that way, walked into the night, and started to send a text as I walked. I stopped texting when I literally bumped into Banko Juarez. He had his laptop perched in an open palm, held before him. His other hand was cupped beside his etheric vibrator thing.

I said, "Either this is an eerie coincidence or—"

"It's 'or,'" he said urgently. "We have to get you out of here."

"Why? And how'd you know I'd be here?"

"The lines," Banko said, as he backed against a tree, pulling me with him. He tapped some keys, then watched the exit anxiously. "I was in the park again and picked up one of those lines we'd been studying, followed it here."

"Which one?" I asked.

He showed me the computer. There were two lines virtually identical.

"Whose is it?" I asked.

"The gal from the hotel," Banko said. "The one on the night desk."

"Maybe she's a student," I said.

"Or maybe she's been following you," Banko replied.

"Can you tell where she is?"

"The etheric reader is not a directional device," he said. "Maybe one day."

I was glad I hadn't sent the text I was about to send. I sent a different one. "I'm going back inside."

"Probably a good idea," he said.

We hustled back toward the door, along with a handful of students who were going to night classes. Including the one who put something hard against my back. It wasn't a frozen knish.

"Don't turn around and don't try to run," someone whispered hotly, hoarsely in my ear. "Just go where the gun points."

It was either a very butch woman or an effeminate man, I couldn't be sure. I couldn't even tell if it belonged to one of the Chinese I'd met. In short, I knew nothing—other than I hoped I lived long enough to apologize to Grant for not taking his advice.

The gun nudged me around the building across the neatly clipped lawn. There were no students here.

"Banko, you there?" I said in a frightened voice.

"Shut up."

That did not come from the guy directly behind me. So there was someone else. Banko had obviously bailed, the craven little *putz*. The pistol walked me along Alameda to another building, Hale Hall. It was a dormitory. I resolved I was going to say something to the man at the desk—until he locked eyes with whoever was behind me and, stone-faced, simply nodded. And I mean simply: the guy barely looked up from his tablet.

I was led to a door. A hand reached around me and knocked: tap-tap-tap, pause, tap-tap. The door opened on a room that would have made Jefferson Davis smile.

I'm not one of those bleeding hearts who thinks that everyone who raises a Confederate flag is a racist or wants to see the nation return to slavery. Some people are genuinely proud and nostalgic for the finer qualities of antebellum living. That said, this room did not belong to one of those individuals. Because right above the bed to my right were the Stars and Bars—while to the right was the big, ugly banner of the Third Reich. Scattered around the room were other pieces of whites-only memorabilia, including posters from various supremacist groups. Including this one: the SSS.

There was only one person in the room. He was a short but massively muscled student with a Marine-style haircut. He shut the door behind me. The gun was lowered. I turned warily and saw another student like the first—and Banko Juarez. The lying *momzer* closed the computer and laid it on the bed under the swastika. There was a rifle case on the bed and, beside it, a box of ammunition.

"So you're a pimp *and* a murdering scumbag," I said.

"I'm just the procurer, as you suggest. These gentlemen are the killers. And you," he chuckled, "are a blind, dopey bitch. You bought my act! You kept coming at me and coming at me, and each time I denied it you believed me!"

"Yeah. I still occasionally make a mistake and trust men."

"You were so easy," he said, still chuckling. "Oh, and that wasn't Bananas' line on the computer. It was *your* line. How do you think I tracked you here?"

"Ah, good," I said. "So the technology works. I'm actually a little glad not to have been duped by every damn thing."

"It works," Banko said. "And the more I refine it, the more I'll be able to find Jews and Muslims. The blacks—they're easy enough to find."

"So what do you do?" I ask. "Go from city to city targeting defenseless people?"

"Truthfully, I'm just getting started," he said. "The etheric readings are a good cover, and they provide useful field work. I am curious, though.

How did you figure out I was working with the girls at the hotel?"

"You don't expect me to tell you that, do you?"

"Sure do," he said flippantly.

One of the muscular students had come up behind me and grabbed my wrists. I struggled for about a second. His fingers were like big, strong tree roots. His companion, the one with the gun, stuffed a ball-gag in my mouth. I realized then that instead of sassing Banko I should have been screaming, in the off chance someone in the dorm might have come to my rescue. Who knew this was going to happen?

The guy who plugged my mouth put his fingers on my scalp and rested a thumb in my left eye. This was not good.

"I want to know who else knows about my business and how they found out," Banko said. "I'm going to name some names, and you are going to stamp your right foot like a horse. One stamp for yes, two for no. If you are slow in responding, my colleague will start to press your eye inward. Eyeballs don't hold up well under pressure, so I suggest you tap dance quickly. Any questions? Please stomp your answer." He smiled smugly at that.

In all the years with my husband, on Wall Street, being duped down here by people who knew the turf better than I did—with all that, I had never known humiliation as intense as I did when I raised and lowered my foot once like a

Lipizzaner. Once, as he had instructed. I knew, of course, that this interview would be quicker and easier if he just took the gag out and asked me for a name. I don't know if I would have given it, but I gathered that this was part of his Aryan fun: humiliating the Jew. The woman. He obviously didn't have any regard for members of my gender except as profit centers.

I wished that Richard Richards had missed me right away and gone looking for me. He probably hadn't even noticed I was gone, or if he did, he figured I went to the lavatory. At least I was right not to worry about being with him.

Some consolation, I thought as Banko moved in closer.

"Detective Daniels," he said.

His little game had started. I tapped my hoof twice.

"Detective Bean."

Another two taps.

"Agent Bowe-Pitt."

Ditto, ditto.

A question occurred to me, then. I was wondering: if I ratted on who knew, did I get to live? That seemed pretty important. But I couldn't exactly raise my hand to ask it. It was sad that in some ways my life hadn't really advanced much beyond first grade.

"Who's left?" Banko wondered aloud. "Yes. The other policeman. What was his name? Richards?"

I hesitated. The thumb pressed down.

Growing up, hearing the stories about concentration camps, I always wondered how I would stand up in a situation where I was starving or freezing or being walked to my death or being tortured. I had no illusions about my capacity to endure pain, from earaches as a kid to toothaches now. It was low. I always imagined I would probably go psychologically numb. But that wasn't what happened.

I stomped my foot. Twice, for no. As scared as I was, I was also angry. The pressure remained on my eye. I started to see swirling, oily black and orange shapes. I was breathing hard through my nose. But above all, I was filled with a kind of rage—and outrage—I had never known before. It didn't make me brave, it made me crazy.

Banko moved closer. "Why did you hesitate about Richards? Because you're lying?"

I tapped twice, quickly. I felt my *tuchas* vibrate—and not from the tapping.

"Richards had access to my computer," Banko said. "Are you sure it wasn't him?"

I tapped twice, trying to make my toe sound bored with the question.

"Let's assume that's true," Banko said. "I'll find out soon enough. Are you trying to buy time? If so, that is a waste of *my* time, and it will cost more than the sight in one eye. Mr. Richards is giving his lecture—one of our people is in there now, learning. You see, we are a well-educated group. Not like the stereotype." He nodded at the man behind me, who released my eye but did not remove his thumb. "So, again. Are you trying to buy time?"

I tapped once.

Banko brightened at the admission. Then he frowned. He glanced back at his computer and lifted the lid. "If you're waiting for your police or FBI friends, they are not in range—and are not likely to be," he said. "They were not near you outside, and they wouldn't know where to find you inside."

I tapped twice, unsolicited.

"You are agreeing with me?" Banko said, surprised.

I tapped twice.

"Then you are waiting for someone else?" Banko suggested.

I tapped twice.

He smiled. "Gwen Katz, I *like* this game!" he enthused. The other two *schlubs* were unmoved.

Banko backed away. He glanced from me to the computer, then back at me. "There are no familiar lines. Who do you think is coming? One of your waitstaff?" He shook his head slowly. "I have their lines. They're not here. The big woman who manages the cash register? I have her line too. Who, then?"

As if on a magical, wonderful cue, I heard something go *whump* in the hall. It wasn't a familiar noise, like someone dropping a book or slamming a door. It had a fatty quality to it. Just like a body hitting the ground.

Banko and the others heard it too. The etherical cleanser nodded at the guy who had his thumb in my eye, the brute with the gun, to see what was up. The big guy strode to the door, cracked it, looked out.

Then came flying back toward me like a cannonball.

Chapter 22

Limbs buckled and bodies whirled.

It happened so fast that Banko didn't have time to react before one of those bodies, the one that answered the door, bowled him over like a duckpin. He landed hard on the computer that was lying on the bed.

I just stood there with a ball-gag in my mouth. My hands were free, but it took me a moment to realize that the man who had been holding me was no longer behind me. He had gone to help his friend, who went flying when the door opened. I saw a leg come through the door, the bottom of a sole find the burly man's face, the round white head snap back hard, and then the flurry of punches and cries that sent the young racist to the cheap carpet.

A young man came straight in. That was the thing that had stunned me about the attack. It was perfectly straight. Dressed in jeans and a TSU sweatshirt, the attacker came through the door, shouting these wild cries like you see in martial arts movies. He knocked bully number one down with a straight-from-his-sternum series of punches, then kicked and walloped thug number two out of the way. In about two seconds, maybe three, he stood before me, the king of the *zetzes*.

It's pretty sad that, even when he was undoing the ball-gag, I knew him only as "the guy who had a TSU sticker on his bicycle."

"Thank you," I wheezed, as he dropped the B&D toy to the floor.

He nodded sharply, turned to Banko. Thug number one was trying to get up, but he went back down when, without even looking at him, the martial artist placed a side kick in his jaw. I didn't bother to shut the door. Other students had begun to gather in the hallway. A few cheered softly; some applauded. A couple took cell phone pictures.

I put myself between them and my savior. If there were other members of the SSS, I didn't want them to know who had beaten up their comrades. I did that while I was shutting the door. The guy who answered it had been knocked far enough inside the room that I didn't even have to move his legs to do that. He had also been knocked hard enough that his jaw was already discolored. Broken, I guessed.

No more hate speech for a while, I thought with satisfaction.

The quick glance I'd had down the corridor

also told me that the monitor wasn't in much
better shape. He lay sprawled like a broken jar
of mayo, all white and drippy and still kind of
collapsing rather than actually moving.

I turned back toward my trembling, wriggling
captor. I picked up the rifle case that was beside
him and set it against the head of the bed.
Banko really did look like a carp on a hook. I
had seen men afraid of Jewish women in my life,
most of them cowed and some of them even terrified, but I had never seen a man so desperate.

"Don't hurt me!" Banko wailed as the young
man picked him up by the front of his shirt. "I'm
not part of this group!"

I walked over to the twin bed. "Let me guess,"
I said. "You're just the IT guy."

"Right! That's right!"

"I should make you clap," I said.

"What?"

"Clap once for yes, two for no. Like a trained
seal, you miserable, rotten bigot."

"I'm not!"

I moved my face closer to his. The martial
artist helped by pulling him up higher. The kid's
balance was amazing; he adjusted his knees
slightly, lowered his center of gravity, and was
able to life the dirt bag higher.

"*A klog is mir,* what was I thinking?" I said.
"You're just a misogynist who makes money from
women who sell their bodies and likes humiliating those who don't. That taste in my mouth
isn't plastic, it's Gulden's!"

"No, no, I'm not like that at all!"

I sneered but refrained from spitting. I pulled the computer out from under him and tossed it onto the other bed. I looked at the young man who was holding him. "What's your name? Or should I just call you the Lone Ranger?"

"Christian," he said.

That was almost funny, under the circumstances.

I looked around, found the ball-gag, and stuffed it in Banko's mouth. "I've heard enough for now. Let's just keep him here till the police arrive."

Christian snapped off Banko's belt, flopped him on his face, and tied his hands behind him. I asked him if he were sure he wanted to stay. He said he did. I hoped he didn't get in trouble for his heroics. When I texted Maggie from the car and asked if she had a guardian angel she could send over, I hadn't actually thought I would need one. Now I was not only glad but also humbled. The lessons Lung Wong had taught him, had given his own life for, were clearly something very special.

And it was pretty clear, now that I thought about it, that Lung Wong *had* died protecting me. It was that thought which kept my soul from sinking as I looked at the Nazi flag tacked to the wall above Banko.

I was sure someone outside had already called the police. I was surer when my tush vibrated again. I looked at my phone. The previous message was from Maggie, telling me that help was just a few steps away. The new message, a voice mail, was from Grant. I texted Maggie first, blessing her from the bottom of my *kishkes* and thanking her, before I called Grant back. I had a good idea what he wanted.

"Yes," I said. "The nine-one-one is about me."

"I'm en route," he said. "Are you all right?"

"Thanks to one of Ken Chan's students I am."

The call was interrupted by the arrival of campus security. I hung up on Grant and was instantly alert as I recognized the faces of the men who stood outside the room. This looked like it would be round two . . . but that worry existed only for a moment. The sadness in the eyes of the foremost guard—the name on his tag said Baker—was not quite like anything I had seen in our previous encounter. He bent low over the student who had opened the door. He felt his neck for a pulse, then bent low to listen to him breathing. The other two guards stood behind him, motioning students to move along. Christian stood beside me, on alert, lithe and strangely fluid as a cobra.

Baker asked one of the other men to call for an ambulance. "I don't want to move them to the infirmary until they've been checked out," he said. The guard then noticed the handgun on the floor. He sighed, rose slowly. His eyes shifted to me and to my guardian. What he said next was as surprising as anything I'd heard since my female gym teacher hit on me: "I'm sorry this happened to you."

Christian didn't relax his stance—the gun was still on the floor, still within reach—but I did.

"Thanks, but why?" I asked.

"This is my son Vince," he said. "We were looking for him that night when you were in the park. I knew he was into this crap and might have been attending one of their secret rallies on campus, but I had hoped—" Baker's voice stopped suddenly as his eyes took in the room. "I had hoped he wasn't being influenced by this other cracker. Apparently, I was mistaken."

"You knew about the German flag?" I asked.

Baker nodded. "I didn't like it. But I also didn't want to push him away. I wanted him to have somewhere to turn."

"Is he . . . I mean, do you think he—?"

"Is he the gunman?" the guard asked when I couldn't quite get it out. "That's not his rifle," he nodded to the other side of the room. "I pray he is not." Now his eyes shifted to Banko. "Is that the guy who was seated with you in Hadley Park?"

I nodded.

"Is he behind this?"

"More than likely," I said.

Banko yelled into the ball-gag. The guard looked at me curiously.

"He had that in my mouth," I explained. "How's the hall monitor—the one who didn't stop the boys when they brought me in with a gun at my back."

"He's unconscious," Baker said. "Lots of blood around his nose."

"There is a police baton beneath him," Christian said. "He attempted to use it."

"Yeah," Baker said. "Colin isn't very perceptive."

I heard sirens outside. Baker stepped back in time to see the police enter the corridor. Grant paused in the doorway only long enough to make sure he didn't contaminate any evidence when he stepped in. Another detective I didn't know remained in the hallway, directing police to start gathering students for interviews.

Grant's expression was one of earnest concern. I was glad to see it, and him. I took a moment to gather my wits and turn to Christian.

"I can't thank you enough for what you did," I said. "Sorry you had to get caught up in this."

"I didn't 'have to,'" he said. "It was my choice. And it was the right one."

There was nothing sentimental about what he said. Nothing personal. I could have been a stranger or an abused dog. But he *had* come running and put himself in harm's way. That was all that really mattered.

"I'm going to wait in the hall," he told Grant as he stepped around him.

Grant nodded as he himself stepped around the two men, who were beginning to stir. He took me to the back of the room, by the window, to make room for the medics. He also wanted to keep an eye on Banko, who was wiggling around and groaning.

"So this is the SSS," he said. "Your catch, your trophy."

"I would rather it not have been," I said.

"I'll have Detective Nørgaard take it all down. I just wanted to make sure you weren't hurt."

"Maggie Chan had one of the kids from the martial arts school keeping an eye on me," I said. "It was hairy, but only for a little while."

His mouth turned slightly on one side. "For all you knew, he might have been one of the people who abducted you."

"I trust Maggie," I said. "I don't think that was her doing."

"It wasn't," Grant said.

"What?"

"We were just about at the bottom of that when we got the bulletin about the attack here," Grant said.

"You going to share or torture me?"

"For now? Torture. I'll be able to tell you a little more when Detective Bean gets back."

"Where'd she go?"

"I'll tell you that, too—later."

Just then, the giant milk pudding of an FBI agent appeared in the doorway. He was togged-out in his biker look for his gig at the hotel. He looked in with an expression of satisfaction.

"So we've got them both," he said, looking at Banko. "I just arrested his partner, Bananas Bundy. She admitted being a stand-in for the gunman on the roof of the building across from the deli. They knew the window would be reflecting glass then and needed a mock target. They also know it would be tough to see *out* then, giving them cover."

"What made her fess up?" I asked.

"I found news chopper footage when I went to check on what Candy Sommerton may have shot," he said. "It was a totally routine traffic report, but when we processed the image, there she was without her wig." He turned to Grant. "She also admitted that she had fingered your officer, Marcuz Frank, to the SSS because he was harassing their brothel. Mr. Juarez here recorded his lines and tracked him to where he and his girlfriend were parked. When we go over the books, I think we'll also find that the hotel was the source of financing for the group."

"Hookers and neo-Nazis, a class operation from top to bottom," Grant said to Banko, who was no longer struggling but just lying there, deflated. This was a guy as *famisched* as they came.

As if more evidence were needed, Bowe-Pitt remarked that the only African-American employees at the hotel seemed to be hookers. My guess, and that of the G-man, was that there would be an investment group somewhere in the shadows that took them to other white supremacist groups.

I went out in the hall to the rec room, where the police were setting up on the tables to take statements. As I walked into the spacious room,

Richard Richards came running in. His face was flushed from running, but it was big and open and strangely *happy*. He was actually smiling by the time he reached me.

"I just heard on my radio," he literally blurted out. "Then you didn't throw in with that whoremaster!"

"Me?" I asked. In the time it took to enunciate those two letters, the clouds cleared and the sun shone down, and I understood Richard Richards and his sudden standoffishness. "You thought I was involved with criminal activities?"

"You kept on hanging with a guy who—you saw, right there on his computer—had a stable of fillies."

That was so endearingly bizarre I didn't even know what to say. I guess I would forever be Gwen Katz of Manhattan: it never occurred to me that someone would be so morally offended by me that he would turn on the ice. But here was that man, acting as though I'd just walked off a C-130 after two years' deployment in Afghanistan.

"I was just helping to find some killers," I told Richards. "God, I sold my interest in the hooker hotel months ago."

That stopped him short. I actually had to tell him I was kidding.

But now it was my time to talk to the tall, warm hunk of Danish named Detective Casper Nørgaard, who had the kind of blond hair and blue eyes that would have been the envy of

Banko Juarez and his crew. For fifteen minutes, though, he was mine. And it was a happy quarter hour of telling him everything that had happened, despite the wedding band and a reference to one of his kids asking if she could take classes at the Po Kung Fu martial arts school.

Sometimes, just plain normal was just plain satisfying.

Chapter 23

Grant conferred with Richards while I gave my interview. Like Detective Bean, Detective Nørgaard used an iPad. With voice recognition. I spoke, it transcribed. I signed the tablet and was done.

Thinking of Detective Bean, I couldn't help but think how she would be sorry she'd missed this big bust. I told Grant to give her my thanks for her part in this.

"You can tell her yourself," he informed me.

Although it was probably safe to pick up my cats and go home now, that was not where I was headed. Because Grant still had work to do, Richards agreed to bag the rest of his class today and give me a lift—to Po Kung Fu Academy.

The ride from TSU was quite different from the ride we had taken earlier. Richards was open, chatty, and smiling. I was actually kind of annoyed; I was the same person I'd been two hours ago, but his perceptions were different.

Everything about our dynamic had been out of my control and based on a fiction. And people wonder why I'm cynical about dating. Besides, my mind was back at the dormitory with Detective Nørgaard. It was good to have a pure girl crush, even if it wasn't going anywhere.

Richards did not know why we were headed to the school, since Grant had not shared that information. But I had a good idea what was up when we arrived. Through the window I saw Detective Bean and several cops. I saw a woman I did not know; she had an infant in her arms. I also saw Maggie holding the hand of a man I had not laid eyes on before. It didn't take a detective to know who that might be.

Richards waited outside, in his car. As I walked in, all eyes turned toward me. The ones I saw first, the ones that were like black olives in a salad, were those of Aunt May. She, and a young man beside her, were in handcuffs. Those eyes held me only for a moment, however, as Maggie came between us, pulling a tall older man toward me.

"They told me you were all right," she said, with open, honest relief.

"As all right as I ever get," I smiled, as she embraced me lightly.

My genetic self-deprecation was lost in the chasm between the cultures. Maggie stepped back, drew the man forward, and said, "Ms. Katz, this is my husband, Ken Chan."

Ken Chan was nearly six feet tall, slender, with

gray hair worn in a crew cut and a long, tranquil face creased with experience and age but not in a way that suggested wear and tear. Just wisdom.

"I'm honored," I said sincerely, shaking his hand.

He smiled warmly and bowed slightly. "You have done a great service to our family."

That puzzled me. A lot. I had gotten the fake Ken Chan killed—because, clearly, he *had* seen the gunman, possibly in the napkin holder, possibly blocking the sun as he rose to take his shot. Lung Wong had acted to protect me.

"I'm not sure what good I could possibly have done . . . ," I said, and then my eyes drifted to Auntie May.

Detective Bean had followed the Chans over. She took me by the arm and walked me toward the door.

"May Wong is the one who abducted you," Bean said. "She and one of her sons."

"Why?"

"To make sure you didn't know that Lung was impersonating the real Chan."

"But she told me about Lung the next day."

"It seemed she was afraid that the truth was starting to come out anyway, and she needed allies. If she let you in on the 'secret,' she might win your sympathy, " said Bean. "All of this was about limiting the size of her financial exposure. If Lung could not be found before the triads were broken in Chinatown, she was off the hook for the wife and child."

"How much could that have cost her, given the price she's going to have to pay now?"

"She's facing fifteen to sixty years for this. She just fessed up to more, though, which I suspect is her way of plea bargaining."

"More—about what?"

"She was heavily invested in massage parlors in Chinatown, which got hit hard during the recession. She also lost a bundle with a broker up there," she looked at her iPad, "fellow by the name of Sammo Biau."

I grinned. "That little *dreykop*," I said. "She had an office near his, denied having known him. I knew she was lying. He was a big *macher* in that hood."

"I have no idea what you just said, but I'll want to talk to you about it—in English."

I shook my head sadly. "So she was in debt, and one or two kids and spousal support arrangements would have put her under."

"Just one of them was a burden she couldn't handle."

I knew that feeling, not from my own finances but from people around me who got hit hard in 2008. That "common wisdom" about Wall Street having sucked dough from the wallets of Main Street was pure fabrication. Despite what the politicians said as they tossed cash at the too-big-to-fails and union businesses, everyone got hurt except for those institutions.

Bean continued. "When it became clear that the school was a target, I called the NYPD to find out what I could about calling off the New York connection. They put me in touch with Chan."

"So it was you who called him from the NPD."

"Correct. I urged him to get back here, since it was possible his wife and students were potential targets of the Muis, the gangsters, or the SSS—it really didn't matter at that moment. All that mattered was that someone was gunning for them. He agreed to come back as soon as he pulled the trigger on a gang leader he was following."

I looked away from Bean. "So are the woman and child Lung's from New York?"

She nodded.

"I don't get it," I said. "He helped take down the triads—*and* he brought the widow and child down here?"

"Point of honor," she said. "He is doing what Lung would have wanted. If he didn't have to join the family business, Lung would have stayed in New York and supported her."

"I like this honor thing," I said.

Bean agreed. "He's a special man. When he heard about the shooting, about the danger to his family, he stayed focused on what he needed to get done at that moment before coming back. Maggie was even cooler. She knew too that whoever the target was, she had to hold this end together."

"That was why she was calling from pay phones," I said. "In case the triads had someone down here, listening or watching."

Bean nodded.

The detective went back to where Auntie May was being held. I decided it was time to go. I would come back some other time, to thank Maggie again and hopefully fill the order Lung Wong had placed for the postponed belt test.

I walked into the night and thanked Richards for waiting, but told him I'd like to walk back. He asked if I was sure. I told him I was. He said he really wouldn't mind taking me back. I didn't tell him to take his puppy-dog enthusiasm and Sunday school morality and *shtup* it. I just started walking.

I was feeling lighter and better than I had in a long time. It wasn't just having the sniper off my back and my kidnapper heading off to prison. I felt as though the last few days had also been an emotional crucible. I wasn't sure what, if anything, had actually been solved. I was still happily estranged from Grant, suddenly disinterested in Richards, and suffering teen-like palpitations from that *shagetz* love god back at the dorm.

I guess that was the point. Nothing had been solved, but I was still smiling.

For me, that was a pretty big victory.

Here is one more of my uncle's magical recipes. Remember: It is printed here exactly as he wrote it all those years ago.

POTATO KNISH

(Usually for words that begin with a K and an N, the K is silent. Kind of like my cousin Hamish, who can never get a word in edgewise when his wife Lillian is talking, which is most of the time. Anyway, with knish, the K is not silent—like Lillian. So the right way to say it is "ka-nish," not "nish." What the heck, say it any way you want.)

Preparing Time: 30 minutes

Cooking Time: Another 30 minutes

Dough must be chilled 2 hours. Put it in the refrigerator if you have one. If you ain't got one, don't come crying to me.

Total Time To Make a Ka-nish: 3 hours

What You Get: About 24 Potato Knishes

Ingredients:

<u>Knish Dough:</u>
8 ounces softened unsalted butter
8 ounces softened cream cheese
½ cup sour cream
3½ cups all-purpose flour
1 teaspoon salt

Potato Filling:

6 large potatoes, peeled, cut into chunks, boiled, cooled and shredded in a grinder. Ain't got a grinder? Call Cousin Bernard, who weighs 400 pounds. He'll come and sit on them.

1 pound onions, chopped and sautéed

2 large whole eggs, beaten

¼ cup instant potato buds

2 teaspoons salt

¾ teaspoon ascorbic acid or vitamin C powder (what, they shouldn't be healthy?)

1 teaspoon garlic powder

1 tablespoon tobasco sauce

8 ounces finely shredded Cheddar cheese (optional—use the cheese or don't use the cheese. What's it to me?)

Egg Wash:

1 large egg beaten with 1 tablespoon water

Preparation:

Use a food processer to prepare the knish dough, then process the butter, cream cheese and sour cream until it's nice and fine. Add flour and salt and smoosh them altogether. Place dough on a sheet of plastic wrap, then flour your hands, roll it into a ball, and wrap securely. It's best to refrigerate at least 2 hours or overnight.

For potato filling, mix together all the ingredients in a large bowl.

Preheat oven at 350 degrees. Meanwhile, flour a cutting board and knead dough into it. Cover with plastic wrap and let rise for 15 minutes. (Hey, I didn't say this would be easy, did I?)

Roll the dough until it reaches about a ¼-inch width. Cut the dough into 3-inch squares using a really sharp knife. Use 1 beaten egg mixed with 1 teaspoon of water and apply egg wash to the squares. Place two dollops of filling onto each square, and wrap the ends under.

Line a baking pan with parchment, brush knishes with egg wash, and place on pan. Continue with rest of dough and filling. Bake for roughly 20 minutes. Knishes work well as an appetizer, side dish, or main course. Mostly, though, they go best with a corned beef or pastrami sandwich.

Suggestion: have some Alka Seltzer ready. We have a saying:

> Deli food is nice
> But you will pay the price
> Your belly it will roar
> Your insides will be sore
> So never ask the question
> You're gonna get indigestion

GREAT BOOKS, GREAT SAVINGS!

When You Visit Our Website:
www.kensingtonbooks.com
You Can Save Money Off The Retail Price
Of Any Book You Purchase!

- All Your Favorite Kensington Authors
- New Releases & Timeless Classics
- Overnight Shipping Available
- eBooks Available For Many Titles
- All Major Credit Cards Accepted

Visit Us Today To Start Saving!
www.kensingtonbooks.com

All Orders Are Subject To Availability.
Shipping and Handling Charges Apply.
Offers and Prices Subject To Change Without Notice.